NICHOLAS KNIGHT'S

NIGHTSHADE

BOOK 3

MOON RIVER

The Nightshade Series, Book 3

NICHOLAS KNIGHT

Burning Bulb

PUBLISHING

Moon River
By **Nicholas Knight**
Burning Bulb Publishing
P.O. Box 4721
Bridgeport, WV 26330-4721
United States of America
www.BurningBulbPublishing.com

Cover designed by Klem Kanthesis.

First Edition.
Paperback Edition ISBN: 978-1-948278-02-7

Printed in the United States of America

PREFACE

In the first book, *Dawn's Tale*, we were introduced to Dawn Moon, a young Cherokee who's institutionalized in a psychiatric facility, in late 1970s Virginia. It's here that she falls madly in love with a much older ginger named, Reuben. She tragically suffers an unbearable trauma that leads her to escape, as well as launch a quest for retribution, which molds her into a serial killer.

In, *Dark Fugitive*, Dawn is on the lam, running and hiding from the FBI. As she continues to dig her hole even deeper, she befriends an abused white wolf, and hooks up with an exotic succubus hybrid who behaves more like an energy vampire, who seduces her into an exceptionally passionate, yet detrimental, lesbian relationship. While all this is happening, Dawn also draws the attention of a brutal coven of Satanic witches who are obsessed with both Lady Isis and Aleister Crowley.

This magical and mystical story will promise to both disturb you and warm your heart. Though this trilogy is about a female werewolf, this is very much a story of uninhibited passion, undying love, and animalistic rage. This book series is a phenomenal one, which I am considerably proud of and surprised to have written.

Thank you for supporting this trilogy, and for getting to know these characters who have come to mean so much to me.

See how Dawn's cautionary saga, her traumatic story, and her very tail...ends! For better or for worse! See Dawn in a new light, as you've never seen her before! Love comes in many forms, and doesn't always make sense. In the rarity that love is true, there is nothing more beautiful! For those reading this, who get their joy from abusing, fighting, and murdering animals...your day will come (if God is good). Enjoy the anticipated finale of this amazing, coital trilogy. Take a dip into *MOON RIVER*!

DEDICATIONS

For Erica Linnette Heath: "You are perfect, as our Father in Heaven is perfect." (Matthew 5:48). "God is love" (1 John 4:8), and so are you. They say you never forget your first love, and you are my truest and greatest love. As I have told you before, baby, love is not a big enough word…it's just not a big enough word…when it comes to what you mean to me and how I feel about you. Philippians 4:8 says we should *think on that which is true, noble, right, pure, lovely, and admirable*, and you, my love, are all those things and more. You were always so humble and gentle, and graciously continue to love me in spite of my flaws and failures (Ephesians 4:1-3). Thank you, Erica, for all of the influence and guidance that you have so kindly, and generously, contributed to this book series. Thank you for taking me back, for still wanting me, for not giving up on me, and for loving me as much as I love you. 1 Peter 1:22 tells us to love with a complete and sincere heart, and you and I are the definition of that. I adore you, Erica, and will always be here (and there) for you. I will always defend your honor, and will forever be yours. You are my hope for Heaven (Hebrews 11:1). You *are* my Heaven. (In Very

Loving Memory, February 22, 1980 – December 27, 2002).

For Harley Linnette Delorie: Though your mother's adopted parents adopted you when you were 10, you will always be my daughter. I adore you and am so proud to be your Dad. I'm sorry that things turned out the way they did. I never wanted us to be a broken family, and I know you're not thrilled about the situation either. I wanted to be with your mother, and I certainly wanted to keep you. Andrea had different plans and other intentions. I've never had luck with women, always attracting the ones who wanted to hurt me. Erica has been the only exception to that, and Jennifer has been the only one to apologize for that. You, Erica, and Rose (your older sister who we lost to a miscarriage) will forever own my heart. I love you, Harley girl, and miss you every day that we're apart. I pray that you understand things someday and know that I tried my best to fight for both you and Andrea. One of the toughest lessons in life is having to accept that we can't make somebody we love, love us back. You were only 2, when Andrea proudly and shamelessly took you from my arms. Part of me died that day, just like part of me died when Jennifer left me and Erica passed away. Those were the three worst days of my life, and certainly the most painful. My love for you, Erica, Jennifer, and Rose, will never die. The majority of Christians are frauds, and the cruelest people you will ever encounter. The reason why I have always been an underachiever (which I am deeply sorry for), is because nobody has ever given me a shot at being anything more (especially those who profess to be "Christian"). Jesus loves you, almost as much as I do. Please stay with God, despite what "Christians" say and do to turn you away from Him. As precious as this life can be, it's not nearly as important as the afterlife. Please don't let this cold world rob you of your faith. I know that you have learned, at such a young age, how toxic and wicked people can be, and I'm so sorry for that. Heaven wouldn't be Heaven without you, Rose, and Erica to share it with. I love you, Harley! Please never forget that.

For Rose Delorie: A "Rose" by any other name is...a daughter. Though you were tragically taken from both myself and Jennifer, I pray that God lets you and I meet one day, in Paradise. Even though I've never had the pleasure or honor of knowing you, I have always...and will always...love you. I sadly wasn't successful at holding onto your beautiful mother, but I have always loved her with great passion and sincerity. You were definitely conceived from love. I'm sorry, Rose, that I didn't include you until this third book. I would have, had I known about you before now.

For Jennifer Lee Hassel: Even if we can never visit each other in person, thank you for being my friend again (at least online). I care for you deeply, and have missed you over these last 25 years. I regretfully failed at keeping you, but I've certainly never forgotten you. I wish you only the best, and pray that life treats you with the kindness that is long overdue and that I've rarely known myself. Thank you for telling me about our daughter, even if it took you this long to do so. I love you, Jennifer, and will always be your friend. I have valued this reconnection you've allowed us to have, even if it must be restricted and transient. I may have lost you to Chris 25 years ago, but you will never lose me. I wish you would let me see you, but I respect your wishes and your reasons. Thank you for reading my books and for permitting me to be in your life again, even if only from afar. Your friendship and support mean a lot to me.

For Tiger: You're the best friend I've ever had. I love you so much. You have never been a pet, but more of a son. You are irreplaceable. You mean so much to me, and I thank both God and Erica for you.

For Kirsten Bergh: Thank you for reading the first book and catching a detail that the rest of us had overlooked. I appreciate your thoughtful feedback.

For Klem Kanthesis: Thank you for contributing this fantastic cover, for the final book in this sentimental saga. Your artwork is absolutely breathtaking, and in retrospect, I wish I had hired you to do all three covers for this trilogy. You really illustrated what was in my head. Thank you, Klem!

For Keira Fox, Kaylynn Coy, Ashley Vierra, and Erin Wrae Sasse: Thank you for wanting to model for this amazing book. Had I been successful at finding a photographer on *Model Mayhem* who wasn't a total dick, I would have loved for you all to have been on this cover. I'm sorry that things didn't work out as we had hoped. You are all very pretty and were very sweet. Thank you for that. I wish we could have worked together.

For Gary Lee Vincent: Thank you for believing in my talent, and for all you've done to support this trilogy and help bring it to life. Thank you for convincing me to make this a series rather than a standalone novel, and for suggesting the initial direction of *Book 2*. Thank you for your friendship, Gary.

For Franziska Schissler: For being the visual inspiration for the look of Dawn's face, on this stunning 3rd cover.

For Russell Clayton Harris, Jr: I'm sorry that our time together was too short and that your life was so painful. You were simply too good for this sordid country. I pray that you are doing well and that you eventually find your way to Heaven, when you're ready to walk into the Light. I love and miss you, Uncle Russ. (In Loving Memory, March 31, 1952 - November 22, 1982)

For Jackie Faircloth: Thank you so much for your unwavering support of this trilogy. I deeply appreciate your kind words regarding my books. You're very talented, and I really hope all of your dreams come true.

For Jay Rizzo: Thank you for being one of two people to ask for my autograph.

For James Crow, Heinz Treschnitzer, and other wonderful friends I've made through my acting endeavors.

For my parents: I love you both, in spite of our differences. I'm sorry that we didn't always relate well, or share much of anything in common. In some ways, I wish I could've been more like you, while in other ways, I'm grateful to be who I am. I appreciate you both always being there for me, in all the ways that you were, but wish that we could have been closer. I'm sorry that it wasn't easy for either of you, and even sorrier that I failed at so much. I have a ton of regret for the bad choices I've made, but most of what has happened to me has not been my fault, as you both well know. This world is full of cruel and sadistic people. Even though we were often at odds, you both are good souls and I am proud to be your son. My childhood was not an easy road, nor has been my adult life, but sometimes I wonder if I could have ever written this magical trilogy, had I not lived the nightmare I have.

For Andy Gibb: I can't resonate to your massive success, but I can most certainly relate to your repeated heartbreak. You were once quoted as saying that it was Victoria (Principal's) callousness and indifference that devastated you the most, and that she made it painfully clear that she felt nothing when she abandoned you. So, though we never knew each other, I definitely feel like we were dealt the same cards, as far as disappointments go. (March 5, 1958 - March 10, 1988)

For every clergyman (and woman), church, politician, girlfriend, wife, corporate head, lawyer, certain extended relatives (who will go unnamed), and others who have kicked me when I'm down, told me I'm worthless and treated me like trash, stepped and spit on my trusting heart, and did everything in their power to wreck and ruin me. Thank you for pushing me to make something of myself and for showing me what I don't want to become. 1 Thessalonians 5:15 warns us to not repay evil for evil, which is why I have always maintained my benignity and my faith, even when presented with animosity, affliction, acrimony, and adversity. Even if these books never make a dime, it won't change my accomplishment or rob me of my sense of pride in creating these marvelous stories. These characters, particularly *Dawn*, *Reuben*, *Cheri*, and *Wolf*, will stay with me forever.

"Life is a process of becoming, a combination of states we have to go through. Where people fail is that they wish to elect a state and remain in it. This is a kind of death."

- Anais Nin

"Shapeshifting requires the ability to transcend your attachments, in particular your ego attachments and identify who you are. If you can get over your attachment to labeling of yourself and your cherishing of your identity, you can be virtually anybody. You can slip in and out of different shells, even different animal forms or deity forms."

- Zeena Schreck

"The self is not something one finds, but rather creates."

- Thomas Szasz

"Since the so-called Age of Enlightenment, our shaky anthropocentric, rationalist egos have been brainwashed to forget what 'primitive' cultures once understood: animals can be manifestations of celestial beings in disguise; they possess supernatural abilities, and they can be our spiritual guides and healers."

- Zeena Schreck

"Beware of the preachers, priests, evangelists, clergymen, and other ministry staff, who come to you in sheep's clothing, but inwardly they are rabid wolves."

- Matthew 7:15

"Life isn't about waiting for the storm to pass, but about learning to dance in the rain."

– Unknown Author

"I believe that the only true religion consists of having a good heart."

- Dalai Lama

"To look into the eyes of a wolf is to see your own soul."

– Aldo Leopold

"Love is the slowest form of suicide. and the most used four-letter word, other than, *life*."

– Dawn Lynne Moon

"When the still sea conspires an armor, currents breed tiny monsters, true sailing is dead and sullen. At night, the moon becomes a woman's face. The sea is a vagina, which may be penetrated at any point. That whorish Blue Lady, playing with silver decks and smiling at the night, and spilled to the moon. I'm sad, so full of sadness. No eternal reward will forgive us now for wasting the dawn."

– James Douglas Morrison

SOME INTERESTING FACTS:

"76% of all known serial killers in the 20th Century, were from the United States."

"Ted Bundy saved a drowning child, and Dennis Rader installed home security alarms for 14 years."

"America's 1st serial killer was Dr. H.H. Holmes, who confessed to killing 27 people in the late 1890s."

"Most serial killers had clean records, Christian reputations, & warned about to police before caught."

"Almost all serial killers admit to starting out by torturing, dissecting, stuffing, and hunting animals."

"44% of serial killers started in their 20s; while 26% started in their teens."

"It only takes 3 murders to earn the title, *serial killer*."

"According to historians, legends such as werewolves and vampires were inspired by medieval serial killers."

"Psychiatrists note that psychopaths are untreatable."

SERIES INTERVIEW

Galina Volkov, a journalist major at *George Mason University*, sat down with Nicholas to interview him for their *Broadside* student newspaper. She wanted to interview him, and give him an opportunity to answer a few questions about his *NIGHTSHADE* Series:

Q: Your writing is very erotic and very dark, more so than most authors? Aren't you worried that you may have damned yourself, by limiting your potential audience by blending these two genres?

Nicholas: There have been plenty of writers who have done this, where they interweaved graphic sex and horror fiction, both in books and in films. In fact, some of the best Horror movies ever made, have been those with graphic sexual content. Is my storytelling a bit more intense and risqué than most? Possibly. But, I find that the extreme always leaves an impression. I don't believe in censorship. I think that, in order for us to say we are a *free country*, we should actually have freedom of expression. When I decided to become a writer, I promised myself in the beginning that I would only write honest stories that offered compelling characters and legendary adventures. So, I intentionally write without limitations or boundaries. Whether you fancy my writing or not, I think you'd have to agree that these novels are hard to erase from your memory, once you've read them. That's my wish…to be unforgettable.

Q: You're not afraid that maybe you go too far, with the erotica?

Nicholas: Let me answer you this way…repression has never worked out well for anyone. History shows this time and again. Repression is what leads priests to molest children. In life, extremes are never a good idea. Too many people are either stuck-up or slutty. Neither one is healthy. Secondly, pornography is not the abomination that Christians make it out to be. Reading or watching porn isn't what damns your soul, your wicked behavior and evil intentions do. Nobody ever goes out and rapes somebody, because they are hooked on pornography. They rape someone, because they're heartless and cruel, two things which come from a place much deeper and darker than any media outlet or entertainment vice. I also don't write smut. Nothing I write is there just for the sake of being there, but rather to enhance and enrich the story. Everything I put into my novels, has purpose and is part of the plan. I should also note that this type of material never hurt anyone. What harms people is things like marriage. This is the one thing that Muslims actually got right. They take infidelity very seriously (not that I condone stoning or beheading anyone), but at least they don't tolerate it. We, in America, not only tolerate it, we enable it and applaud it. If a woman sleeps around on her boyfriend or husband, here in America, she gets full custody and government-funded welfare. We all know the horrible sex crimes that are out there, and if you read my books, you'll see that I don't paint any of them in a good light.

Q: Why werewolves?

Nicholas: It's always bothered me that most of the werewolf movies I've seen in my lifetime have been shit. People love *The Howling* (with Dee Wallace), but I found it a bit silly and rather boring. I did, however, dig the fourth one (*The Original Nightmare*) and the eighth one (*Reborn*). But, the best werewolf movie I've ever seen has been the original *Ginger Snaps* (2000). The two sequels were dreadful and unwatchable, but the first one was great. The majority of werewolf films, though, have been complete garbage. The best vampire movie I've ever seen was a 2009 Horror-Comedy called, *Suck*, which is a brilliant film. I realize you're asking me about a book, not a movie, but they're both mediums of storytelling, and…I'd love to see my 'Dawn' trilogy be adapted onto the big screen (or small screen), but I realize that's a pipe dream.

Matthew 7:15 warns us of wolves in sheep's clothing, but fails to mention that these "wolves" are actually preachers, ministers, pastors, evangelists, and baptized

"Christians." This verse gives wolves a bad name, as wolves are not malicious or sadistic like most humans. Wolves are certainly more altruistic and benevolent than the majority of Christians. Wolves are instinctively loyal to their mates, their pack, and to one another. Wolves don't use or play each other, or pretend to care while secretly harboring cruel intentions. Wolves are protective and genuine. They're not shallow, selfish, scheming, sanctimonious, or sadistic. People view wolves as vicious, tragically giving them the stigma of being malevolent, but this is unwarranted and unfounded. Yet, mankind has brutally hunted them down, to the degree of forever endangering this gentle, magical, and beautiful species.

Q: Why witchcraft?

Nicholas: They say that the greatest authors write what they know, and I happen to know quite a bit about this particular subject. For one reason or another, I have crossed paths with quite a few people who have been involved (or are currently involved) in witchcraft or Satanism. There's a lot of real evil out there in the world, but the scary thing is, it's mostly from Christians, not Satanists. At least with a Satanist, you know what you're getting. With a Christian, you never know what kind of monster you're dealing with. I'm an animal lover and a doting father. I'm also an activist for gun control. I find it unsettling how Satanists respect animals (much like the Native Americans do), whereas many Christians like to stuff them and mount them on their walls. Satanists hold children in high regard, whereas many Christians molest and rape them. The Christian community frowns and scoffs at abortion (which I agree is an indefensible atrocity), but then these same impostors contradict themselves by gathering together and taking joy out of hunting down those who are equally innocent and defenseless. It turns my stomach. Do I admire Satanists? Of course not. Am I an advocate for witchcraft? Not in the least. If you really take the time to read my books, you will see that I don't paint witchcraft or the Christian Church in a good light. My purpose is to expose both.

Q: Yes, I noticed your hostility towards Christianity, in this series?

Nicholas: I have nothing but admiration, love, and respect for Christ. I'm a firm believer in the Lord Jesus and his message. I just don't believe in the Christian church. I believe that the Bible is the infallible, inspired Word of God (by that, I mean, the true Bible – which for us would be the *King James Version*, which is the closest we have to the original texts). It just disgusts me that mankind has rewritten and revised the Bible innumerable times over. The Christian community is full of bullies and frauds who are all about deceit and materialism, which is why they continue to profusely come out with new, alleged *versions* of the Bible, as they do their best to contaminate it a little more each time, throwing in their own so-called *interpretations* and *translations*, to suit their own agenda and propaganda. The Bible was meant to be held sacred and unaltered. (Deut 4:2; Rev 22:18-19) We all know that there were things edited out of the original Holy Bible, not by God, but by man. We just have no way of knowing what those things were. Does that make the Gospel flawed or fake? Of course not. It simply means that it's incomplete and imperfect, which is man's fault, not the good Lord's.

I have no problem with Jesus Christ. It's the majority of Christians who get under my skin. I can't tell you how many condescending bigots and shameless hypocrites I have met, in my lifetime, who were esteemed ministry leaders and revered preachers. I have known more pastors than most people, and not one proved to be sincere or genuine...not one. Every sadistic sociopath who has maliciously attacked me with either malice, infidelity, or other means of betrayal, has allegedly been a baptized *Born-Again Christian*. I've had to learn that there is no such thing as the Christian church. It doesn't exist. The last ones to honor Jesus, are Christians. That's sad to say, but it's true. Finding a Christian, or a church leader, who properly represents Christ, is tougher than finding a needle in a haystack. Christ was never about greed or hate. Christians are. None of us are flawless, but there is a difference between being imperfect and being insincere. I've known a few real Christians…a very few.

Matthew 10:22 and 2 Timothy 3:12 make it clear that Christians (true Christians, that is) will be consistently persecuted. What the Bible neglects to mention, however, is that we will be persecuted by prosperous, abundantly blessed, pseudo-Christians. The Bible tells us that there is a season for everything under the sun (Ecclesiastes 3:1), but it doesn't mention that, for some of us, that season is a lifetime. The Gospel also instructs us to not take revenge, because God will do this on our behalf and pay back those who enjoy harming us (Romans 12:19). The Bible makes a ton of promises like this, most of which never come true. Karma is a nice fantasy, but sadly, that's all it is. Bad people thrive and flourish, while good people get the shaft every time. There's not much *culture* in the *gun culture*, just like there's not much *Christ* in *Christianity*.

Q: I noticed you tend to write about Heaven or Hell, God or Satan. Even the Horror books you write, which wouldn't be sold anywhere in Christian bookstores, have very religious elements to them?

Nicholas: Every story needs a protagonist and an antagonist. Every story needs a hero and a villain. What better than to write about the ultimate in both categories? I actually wrote a Christian novel not long ago (which is the only one I plan to ever write) that is very dear to my heart. It's called, *The Disciple*, and is a wonderful story, which is a very personal project. I had to self-publish it, because none of the alleged *Christian* publishers would touch it or glance at it twice. I tried getting on *The 700 Club*, which is located in Virginia Beach, to promote the book, but they wouldn't even consider letting me come on their show, unless I bribed them with several thousands of dollars.

Q: No. You're kidding?

Nicholas: I wish I was. It was disturbing, but not surprising. By that time, I had already gotten a healthy taste of what the *Christian* filmmakers are like, who are equally as corrupt, counterfeit, fraudulent, and fickle as the Christian publishers out there. I had hoped to be in Christian movies as well, particularly so that my daughter could see some of my films, but the connections I've made in the Horror genre have proven to have far more integrity than any of the so-called *Christian* directors I've encountered. Yeah…trust me…people like Chip Rossetti and David A.R. White are a complete sham.

Q: Your Christian novel is a bit of a departure from what you normally write, isn't it?

Nicholas: Very much so. I have no intentions or plans on doing another one like that. The only reason why I wrote *The Disciple*, to be honest, was to honor my undying love for my daughter and my fiancé. This book was primarily to tribute them, which is why they are both on the front cover and why two of the principle characters are heavily molded after them.

Q: Why the 1970s?

Nicholas: This country has never been a great nation. It breaks my heart to say that, but it is what it is. America has always been a joke, but in the 1960s and 1970s, at least there seemed to be more Americans who understood that, who were troubled by that, and who bound together to fight that fact. I love the music, the fashion, the look, and the feel from that decade. Kids weren't shooting other kids or having kids of their own. It was just another world then, and a better time (well, except for all of the infamous serial killers that were operating during that decade).

Q: You write very strong female characters. Does this come easy?

Nicholas: Strangely, yes, which is quite odd. The vast majority of the women I have been unfortunate enough to know, in my lifetime, have proven to be monsters. I am twice-divorced, have been engaged many times, and have had more girlfriends than I care to admit. Only one of them ever genuinely loved me back, and she wasn't one of the two I regretfully married. I'm amazed that I was able to create characters like *Dawn* and *Cheri*, who are strong and endearing, since most of the females I've encountered in my life are callous and cruel. Most women, especially nowadays, are too shallow and superficial to honestly care about anyone, and too phony and fickle to stay with anyone. What bothers me most, and what I'll never get used to seeing, is how too many women get off on destroying those men they pretend to have loved. There's a reason why there are so many single mothers in this nation, and it rarely has anything to do with abusive husbands or deadbeat fathers (although those men do exist). Dawn and Cheri are both monsters, but they're not heartless, which makes them more fictional than the fact that Dawn is a werewolf and Cheri is a semi-succubus.

Q: Are there any books or movies that influence or inspire you?

Nicholas: Movies, yes. I love John Carpenter's 1994 masterpiece, *In The Mouth of Madness*, which is about a Horror writer. The film, *Dream Lover*, has also been frighteningly autobiographical for me. There have been a few different films with this same title, so I should clarify which one I'm referring to. It's the *Dream Lover* that came out in 1993, starring James Spader and Madchen Amick. There are others, but those two immediately come to mind. I tend to be drawn to films which are uniquely original and irresistibly moving. For example, Milla Jovovich did a film entitled, *Ultraviolet*, in 2006, which is grossly underrated and underappreciated. It's essentially a vampire story, but it is unlike any other vampire story you will find. So creative, so brilliant, and so well done…and, Milla, as usual, is wonderful in it. 2017's *Logan* and 2017's *The Shape of Water* are probably the two best movies I've ever seen in my lifetime, and yes, they both inspired me quite a bit as an artist. As far as books go, *White Fang* really got to me. I love the 1991 film, as well (the much better remake with Ethan Hawke). Beautiful story! I like films that I can personally relate to, and I like writing what I know. Anyone who knows me will tell you that I put a lot of myself into my characters and a lot of truth into my stories.

Q: What audience do you think your *NIGHTSHADE Series* will win over?

Nicholas: I'm often asked what demographic I'm trying to reach, with this series. I guess it's unclear, because of the complexity and diversity of the themes found in this story. The key elements of this story are obviously mental illness, the paranormal and supernatural, traumatic loss, undying love, retribution, lesbianism, and the brutal savagery of the *real* monsters of this world. The trilogy takes place in the late 1970s, so there are historical events weaved into this thrilling saga, for both authenticity and human interest. There are unsettling and controversial subjects like witchcraft, Islam, and other deplorable atrocities.

This story, like it or not, is very genuine and original. It exposes a ton of darkness, in various degrees, but it also teaches some priceless lessons about life, love, and the consequences of our choices. You will also find things like passion and commitment, selfless sacrifice, and hope and redemption. So, all in all, I'd say that this book series speaks to a broad range of readership. You won't find another story like this anywhere, unless of course someone plagiarizes from this, as too many writers are sadly known to do to other authors. This trilogy is *not* intended for children, which goes without saying. I tried to make this concise by illustrating the covers how they are, and constructing the synopses the way I did.

Q: What made you write this trilogy?

Nicholas: It was initially going to be a standalone novel, called *NIGHTSHADE*, but my friend, Gary Lee Vincent, talked me into making it a series. I'm really glad he did, because if he hadn't, *DARK FUGITIVE* and *MOON RIVER* may have never existed, which would be a tragedy, in my opinion. When it was still going to be a standalone story, rather than a saga, I had contemplated using two other titles before deciding on *NIGHTSHADE*. It went from being *DARK BLOOD* to

PRAYER OF THE FORSAKEN to *NIGHTSHADE* to *DAWN'S TALE* (*Nightshade #1*).

Q: Have you had any feedback on this Series, that was pleasantly or unpleasantly unexpected, or that stands out to you in any way? And, if so, how? Why?

Nicholas: After 25 years, I was pleasantly surprised to succeed in reconnecting and reconciling with my original ex-girlfriend, Jennifer Hassel (then, "Jennifer Carter"). She was the first girl I ever gave my heart to, ever got engaged with, and ever got crushed by. It was immensely painful to lose her to the man she immediately married, but it has meant the world to me that she has broken the popular trend that all my other ex's have set…and offered her hand of friendship (at least online), which is the second best thing to having a second chance. Jennifer is someone I deeply wanted, but couldn't have. Though her heart was always with someone else, she was always a special person, which was partly why it was so hard losing her.

As I wrote this third book, to close my Dawn trilogy, Jennifer kindly agreed to read the first two. After finishing the second book, she told me that she had a few nights where she couldn't sleep, but rather tossed and turned over these books. Though this made me feel bad, I also took it as a compliment. She told me that she thinks I'm a very good writer, but what kept her up at night were all the *good things* and *not-so-good things* about this trilogy. I also learned that Jennifer shares my love for wolves, which is a fact that I was unaware of until now. She told me that she actually got to pet and play with one during a visit to a Rescue in NJ, which brought tears of joy and jealousy to my eyes. Thank you, Jennifer, for your forgiveness and for being the only ex-flame who ever apologized for burning me. Thank you for letting me get to know you again, even if it has to be with restriction and only from a distance.

Jennifer: *First I want to tell you what a fantastic writer you are. I read Book 1 and then 2. Phenomenal. There are things I would change. I would've talked more about the asylum and have Reuben stay alive and make him more of the story. I also got confused if Dawn was the wolf or if the wolf was a separate identity? It gets a little confusing. After her killing everyone she was able to escape, which makes me think she is the wolf and maybe she doesn't know it yet? At the end of the first book, police are searching for her, but then in the next story, they couldn't find her, so it seems like they've given up. Then there's another part of a totally different story about the circus and the love between Dawn and another girl. It was this different twist, in the end, that kept me interested. I think that you should focus some more on her being pursued by the cops, more about her Dad, and tie all the stories together. I don't get the* *spiritual stuff in the beginning, but that could be just me. Just a quick note. You are a good writer.*

G: Thank you for letting me interview you today, Mr. Knight. It was nice meeting you. I look forward to reading *MOON RIVER*. I really love the first two books.

Nicholas: I hope you enjoy this final chapter. Seeing this last book published is kind of bittersweet for me. I really love Dawn, even though I realize she's fictional. So, it's a bit hard to see her saga come to an end. But, then again, such is life, right? By the way, you have a lovely accent and your English is very good.

G: Thank you (she says with a kind smile). My parents are Russian, but I, myself, have never lived in Russia. Thank you for treating me to lunch earlier, Mr. Knight.

Nicholas: It was my pleasure, Galina. Thank you for being so sweet, and for being interested in my books. (Nicholas and Galina share a warm hug, and go their separate ways)

{Sadly, Galina's submission to her college paper got unjustly rejected, because the editors-in-charge learned that Nick's *NIGHTSHADE* Series is an erotic one, and didn't wish to promote anything which encompassed sexual content}.

MOON SONG

I raise my arms in greeting
As she slips up through the night
The rounded moon of mystery
A glowing silver disk of light

My spirit answers to her call
And longs for wings to fly
That I might seek her secret place
Whose symbol is the sky

A place of hidden secrets
Of sacred mysteries old
A place I knew in other times
In temple wisdom no more told

I struggle to remember
All the things I learned before
The forgotten mysteries of the moon
The goddess of her lore

Although my arms reach skyward
I turn inward toward her voice
I tread the inner labyrinth
Trusting in my choice

Seek not without, but deep within
The words are soft and clear
Keep faith with me for thirteen months
The mother's sacred year

I watch her through her cycles
As I did in lives before
And follow down her moonbeam path
To the secret, inner door

- D.J. Conway

SMOKE SIGNALS FROM HELL

The Werewolf Order was a magical resistance circle from 1988 to 1999. This was founded by Nikolas and Zeena Schreck, after their stylistically eclectic and classical, LA/European-based collective, *Radio Werewolf*, disbanded. They believed themselves to be the archetypes of the unleashed beast in mankind. Historically, people have been falsely accused of being mythological monsters like this and have been sadistically burned at the stake for it by pseudo-Christians. Those in *The Werewolf Order* believed that they created themselves, and mystically chose and paired their parents, to give them the best genetic-magic possible. They believed themselves to have animal instinct and intuition, and that the werewolf represents strength and power.

In the process of defending the *Church of Satan* from unfounded claims in the U.S. mass media, Zeena's media appearances attracted a new upsurge of membership to the formerly moribund organization, even as she began to question and ultimately reject the self-centered, atheist philosophy she promoted. As she toured the United States on behalf of the *Church of Satan*, Zeena's crisis of faith reached its highpoint when she learned that most of her father's self-created legend was based on lies and many of his works were plagiarized. When jealousy and spite motivated Anton LaVey and his administrator, Densley-Barton, to actually endanger Zeena's life, she could no longer, in good conscience, continue to cover up her progenitor's true character. After serving for some time, in *The Temple of Set*, Zeena and her husband moved to Germany and converted to tantric Buddhism, where Zeena became a respected yogini.

Anton Szandor LaVey died on October 29, 1997, at *St. Mary's Medical Center*, in San Francisco, CA. While on his death bed, moments before his last breath, he was quoted as expressing deep regret for his life of blasphemy. Those who were at his side, at the end, testified that Anton was frantic in terror, as he professed to have seen horrific creatures that were coming for his damned soul.

Nikolas and Zeena Schreck still swear by their werewolf beliefs and identities, but have entirely renounced her charlatan-father's Satanic religion.

I stand accused, I believe in the forces of darkness
An incurable believer in the magic of the midnight sky
And the love that I found today
Oh I can't let it slip away
Oh darling, can't you read between the lines

- Shaun Cassidy

THE MOON

The moon was but a chin of gold
A night or two ago,
And now she turns her perfect face
Upon the world below.

Her forehead is of amplest blond;
Her cheek like beryl stone;
Her eye unto the summer dew
The likest I have known.

Her lips of amber never part;
But what must be the smile
Upon her friend she could bestow
Were such her silver will!

And what a privilege to be
But the remotest star!
For certainly her way might pass
Beside your twinkling door.

Her bonnet is the firmament,
The universe her shoe,
The stars the trinkets at her belt,
Her dimities of blue.

- Emily Dickinson

Time and space only apply to the living, and have no power or authority in the afterlife. In Heaven, 60 years is more like 60 minutes. In Hell, 6 minutes is a lifetime. Time is short on this Earth, and it goes by quickly. We're all running out of time. Be good to each other, and do whatever you can to be right with God.

- A Wise Man

APRIL 13, 1947
FLESHBACK
REUBEN'S BACKSTORY

Reuben spent most of his time sleeping, when he wasn't in school. His parents ragged on him for not having a social life, making him feel strange for not having any friends. They contributed to the demolition of his self-esteem, having no idea what life was like for him. He dreaded each and every morning going to school, not knowing what that day would bring. He had been beaten up in the restroom, his face shoved in toilets, struck with and locked inside lockers, and most recently had his privates taped up during gym class. This had happened in front of the teacher, who just laughed along and let it happen. They had tightly wrapped the tape around that area, effectively covering his penis, balls, and butt cheeks. Reuben had abnormally sensitive skin and tended to bleed easily, so he sat awkwardly in discomfort for the remainder of the afternoon.

On the bus ride home, one of the popular girls, whom he knew was going steady with one of his most vicious bullies, came over and straddled him. They had noticed him shifting his weight in his seat, trying to take pressure off his aching backside, so they sent the class slut to saddle him and keep him still.

"I don't know why nobody likes you?" the teasing trollop told him, resting her delicate forearms on his neglected shoulders. "I think you're a real dish. It's okay," she said, noticing him eyeing her voluptuous bust that barely stayed in her smoked-out blouse. "Take a gander. Get a good eye full, sexy," she said insincerely, further adding insult to injury.

Reuben's anxiety often caused him to shake and sweat. He had also taught himself to speak slowly, as to help keep him from stammering his speech. This broad was considerably attractive, even though she was ugly around the heart.

"What's wrong?" she asked him. "Don't I turn you on? Don't you like boobies?" she asked, smiling, not feeling him grow underneath her. Even if he had gotten stiff, it would have been difficult for her to feel him through the layers of duct tape.

"Maxine, he can't get a boner! Don't you know? Gingers have no pulse! They have no souls!" one of the bullies bellowed out, as the busload of students laughed and mocked Reuben for not getting excited by the hot chick on his lap.

"Is that true?" the mean tramp asked Reuben, who was too scared and shaken-up to respond.

"According to Greek mythology, it is!" Another student blurted out. "It says that redheads turn into vampires, after they croak!"

"He probably doesn't even fancy dollies!" One of the other guys shouted over the collective laughter, at Reuben's expense. The truth was, Reuben found her ass more enticing than her bosom. He could feel her butt cheeks resting on his thighs, which sent a surge of electricity through his veins. He imagined what it would be like to have her sedated and restrained, so he could explore the curves and tunnels of her anal wonderland.

As soon as Reuben made it home, he went straight upstairs to undress and climb into the manganese-stained tub. He decided it would be a safer bet to soak himself in a warm bath, and let the cistern water loosen the tape, so he wouldn't have to pull it off his flesh. His mother was sitting on the sofa when he came through the door, and said 'hello' to him, but was ignored. Reuben thought about suicide an awful lot, but his detrimental fear of death kept him from acting on his desperate tendencies. He couldn't confide in either of his parents, who were incessantly uncaring and insensitive when it regarded him. He would have kept a journal, logging his innermost feelings and secrets, but he knew nobody would ever read it, which debilitated the point for him.

She and his father were devoutly religious, and had taken him to their priest several times, but it never helped. They would catch Reuben keeping things from them and lying to them about the littlest things, never taking any accountability for why Reuben was afraid to be honest and open with them. The last time they had taken Reuben to see Father Paresh, they told the collared clergyman, in front of Reuben, that they felt they must've gotten a bum son, since he was clearly incapable of making friends or attracting dames. They claimed that there had to be something wrong with Reuben, and that it was his fault for being such an outcast. Father Paresh felt increasingly uncomfortable talking to the Petersons, not because they were lousy parents, but because of their syrupy German accent.

Reuben had awoken that morning, after tossing and turning all night in his restless sleep. He came to with crust in his eyes and blood in the back of his underwear. He was a young boy with his whole life ahead of him, yet he felt aged and frail. His poor health was unfairly premature and gradually getting worse, yet no matter how bad it got, he seemed to live in spite of his cursed condition. He got out of bed that morning perspiring, while chilled at the same time. His head pounded in pain just above his eyes, which wanted to go back to sleep.

"Vaht's cooking?" the soused Gerhard asked his subservient wife, as he aggressively cups one of her ass cheeks with his open hand, stumbling by her to sit at the head of the breakfast table.

Helga is wearing his favorite casual, collared shirt, which had a colorful, checkered pattern to it. She didn't have anything on below her waist, not even a single unmentionable. He zoomed in on his wife's gams and thought about the oppression they had barely escaped in Germany. He was grateful to have left the Third Reich behind them, even though you'd never be able to tell it by the manner that he and Helga behaved.

"Vaht vould you like, Daddy?" she asked. "To eggs and bacon sound good?"

"As long as I can eat zem off your sveet ass," he replied back.

"You can haff vatevah you vant, Daddy. You know zat," she said, bringing a smile to his face. "Just keep blowing your vawd on me, or in me." Helga had no filter and not a hint of shame. She said what she felt, and felt what she said, which…unlike her other qualities…was quite admirable and unusual.

"You know I vill, ton't you?" he said to the high-maintenance slut he called his *wife*. They didn't have much, but whenever he had extra moolah to spend, it mostly went towards her materialistic fetishes.

Reuben's bedroom was the cellar, which was darker but much cooler, which Reuben preferred. His parents heard him come up the creaky steps, and as soon as he stepped through the door and into the kitchen, his parents wasted no time in letting him have the earful that he had become so accustomed to expecting from them.

"I see you slept in your dirty clothes again," his mother said, shaking her head in disgust. "Ton't ve buy you pajamas?" she asked rhetorically, as she shamelessly flaunted her lower private parts to her impressionable child. "Ton't ve buy you vat you need? Yet, this is how you zank us, right? Real nice, Reuben." He had fallen asleep in what he had worn the night before, which was a solid black T-shirt and faded blue jeans. This was one of several habits Reuben displayed that she considered to be reprehensible. "And you know I hate it vhen all you vear is black. Vat's vong vif color? Huh? You're too good to vear color, I suppose? Is zat it? You look like a goddam mortician."

"You know your muzah's right, ton't you?" Mr. Peterson asked. "I mean, look at you for Christ's sake. You look like the *Black Death* became a person. It's bad enough zat you're so damned pale, and haff zat repugnant hair lip on your face. You von't let your muzah cut your hair, vhich looks like it was born soaked in blood. The least you could to is tress nice for her, so ve ton't haff to be so damned ashamed." Reuben's father always spoke extra slowly to him, as if to give the impression that he viewed his son as being mentally retarded and incapable of understanding much.

Reuben stood at the bus stop, waiting for the yellow shuttle, with an umbrella to keep the hostile sun off him. He's standing several feet from the rest of the kids, not by his own preference or choice. He can hear them whispering to each other about him, and can feel the girls detest his very existence.

"Nice umbrella," one of the other boys complimented sarcastically. "Trying to impress the chicks there, ace?"

"Give him a break," one of the damsels said with counterfeit compassion. "He's pathetic and sad. He can't help it."

"Yeah, I'll give him a break," another future despot threatened. "If he ever tries to bum my dame, I'll give him a break alright."

The cruel kids laughed at him, as the girls joined in on the fun and hung all over the jerks. When the motor coach finally came, Reuben continued to keep silent and made his way to the back of the bus, where he'd sit alone and had the displeasure of seeing and hearing all the mockery at his expense. The students blew spitballs at him, doing all they could to keep his heart pounding and his head hanging.

After a long morning, it was time for the students to feed their stomachs instead of their minds. Reuben sat alone with his paper bag, as was his routine. He could feel the barrage of gawks and glares from the others in the cafeteria, and could hear their contempt and ridicule. He hung his head in low self-esteem, pretending to look down and not be affected by the cruel callousness of his classmates. The anxious Reuben had only taken one bite out of his dry pastrami sandwich, when he sensed that something was terribly wrong outside. Following his intuition, the social pariah instinctively pushes himself away from the table, and rises from his chair so fast that he leaves it spinning on one leg. The same second that his chair hits the floor, Reuben is out the doors. No more than fifteen minutes later, a few of his peers and a couple of the teachers had formed a circle around Reuben, who was cradling a stray Siberian Husky in his empathetic lap.

"I zink he's dehydrated," Reuben said, trying his best at holding back the tears, but failing miserably. "It's too hot outside."

"Zink?" one of the male teachers asked, sarcastically. "You mean think? Say *think*, boy. Try it. Maybe these other kids would pick on you less if you didn't talk like a fucking Nazi?"

"Hey, Reuben," one of the nicer kids began, "don't worry. Animals are made so that their fur keeps them cool in the heat."

"Shut up, Stanley Stupid," one of the pretty girls said, before shoving him hard enough to knock him off his balance.

Reuben looked over at Stanley, who had fallen flat on his face, and busted both his bottom lip and eyeglasses as a direct result from landing on the pavement. He was tempted to tell Stanley that he had been misinformed, and that the fur only helped protect the dog from the cold and not the heat, but he kept that fact to himself, not wanting to embarrass the nerd any more than they already had.

"Do you haff any vawter?" Reuben begged, putting the dog's suffering before his own. "Please, somebody…give me some vawter so I can help him!"

Reuben's emotional reaction to the limp Husky provoked laughter from everybody but Stanley, who started to sneak away, only to be held back by one of the two spectating teachers.

"Not so fast, boy," Mr. Johnson said quietly, so that only Stanley could hear him, as he secured the back of the geek's collar with his firm grip. He knew that Stanley wanted to do a good deed and fetch some water for the distressed dog, but the rest of the unsympathetic crowd were having too much fun to let that refreshment happen.

Later that same day, the 11-year-old found himself on the dreaded field again, with his fellow 6th graders. It was particularly bright that sunny afternoon, on top of the blistering weather that already made the day miserable on its own. Reuben looked even more gothic in his black, red, and white uniform. He had absolutely no interest in being a part of the *Crosses*, but it was important to his father for him to be there and to be active in these group competitions. Despite being regularly crucified by both of his parents, he still wanted to make his father proud. Gerhard had collected baseball cards his entire life, and had long dreamed that his only son would be a face on one of those cards.

These games were well supported by the parents and faculty of *Divine Grace Academy*, and were considered a big deal by the local population, most of whom were sports-obsessed. Just then, one of the lads on the opposing team hit the ball and knocked it clean into the sky above. Suddenly, the Little League game seemed to be moving in slow motion to everyone there. Mr. Peterson heard the rowdy cheering as he watched the pop-fly head straight toward his son. Gerhard, for the first time, was filled with anticipation and excitement about his boy. Could this be the moment he had been praying for? He started to believe that it was, until Reuben keeled over, holding his stomach, just seconds before the ball dropped not even a foot behind where he stood. As people screamed curses at young Reuben, he collapsed on the neatly-trimmed grass, in sheer physical agony.

Reuben regurgitated mass amounts of blood, after nearly choking on it. He did this right in front of everyone, getting it all over his shiny new cleats and spotless pantaloons, which all cost more money than they should. Rather than be concerned for his troubled and tormented son, Mr. Peterson was furious and embarrassed. Reuben had been complaining to his parents for what felt like forever, telling them about the chronic symptoms that he was having, but they never batted an eye or thought to make an appointment for him to be seen. Reuben suffered from autoimmune disorders, as well as severe porphyria, which included extreme photosensitivity to the sun's rays. However, because it was still undiagnosed, nobody took any measures to protect him from harm or keep him away from risk factors.

When Reuben did this hemo-vomiting, in place of catching the ball that was well within his reach, his selfish and insensitive teammates royally chewed him out for it.

"You really got yourself a winner there, don't you?" one of the other fathers remarked as he intentionally and aggressively brushed Mr. Peterson's shoulder while walking to his car. Mr. Peterson would have knocked the guy out, but this particular parent had a chrome dome and a hell of an arm.

"Applesauce! Thanks a lot, Reuben!" the angry lad said to the ginger with the rat-tail hairdo.

"I know he's your only son, Gerhard, but I think you're whistling Dixie with this one," another one of the fathers said, as he padded him on the same assaulted shoulder while he walked by.

"Fuck!" another boy shouted. "I guess this means no pizza again!" The boys all looked at Reuben as if they were unanimously dying to rub him out.

"Coach can't get us pizza anyways. Remember? Reuben can't have garlic. He's allergic," the boy said in a snide and cynical way.

"Dammit! Why is that loser even on the team?!" another boy cried, joining in on collectively busting Reuben's chops.

Reuben's father found it both ironic and pathetic that the team really joined together to attack his son, yet didn't work so well together on the field. "If you spoiled brats vould put zat same anger into vinning a game now an zen, maybe you vould break your losing streak?" he said under his breath, quietly to himself, careful to not let anyone else hear. Any loving father would have reassured his boy that he was proud of him no matter what, and encouraged him to brush off the beefy bullshit from the other kids, but Mr. Peterson didn't do loving. He was just upset that this made him look bad, which bothered him considerably more than his sick son being ritualistically bullied.

On the drive home, the maladjusted youngster felt like he was riding in the back of a black and white. Reuben had to sit behind his father, in the backseat of the maroon 1946 *Ford* Sedan, since his father couldn't stand the sight of him. Though this wounded Reuben's feelings, he couldn't entirely blame his Dad. As the coal miner drove them back to the dysfunctional house, Reuben caught his ugly reflection in the window and it honestly made him sicker. Reuben's father had planned on taking the Misses to a be-bop that night, after getting a sitter for Reuben, but he somehow didn't feel much like celebrating. The harsh reality that nobody wanted to own up to, was that the team just wasn't that good at athletics. They never won, with or without Reuben, because they were a bunch of unskilled dingbats. They knew that everyone despised Reuben, and also knew that he wouldn't fight back, which made him the perfect patsy and ideal target.

The next day, Reuben is barbarically beaten up by the neighborhood kids, in front of his own house. His mother stands by and watches, wearing her giant, extra-thick spectacles. The kids call him every name in the book, blaming him for not only being hideous and useless, but for also being the offspring of whom they considered to be Nazi rejects. Many of the students who attended his Catholic school, lived there on site. Reuben, however, was not welcomed to stay on campus, even if his parents had been willing to fork up the extra costs to make that happen. People either feared Reuben, or were grossed out by him, purely and solely because of the way he looked. Because he was such a fabled, social outcast, kids knew where to find him when they had the sudden and overwhelming urge to punish him for being him.

"That's what you get, Nazi boy!" one of the Italian kids shouted, as he helped his juvenile posse kick Reuben while he was already down and vulnerable. The kids ganged up on him, forcefully stomping him with all they had, showing neither mercy or restraint.

The majority of the people who lived in or around Johnstown, were of Italian or Polish descent. So, with

Reuben being what he was, he would have been fair game anyway, even if he hadn't been born with a face that the community found repulsive.

"Ve're not Nazis, itiot," Reuben calmly but firmly corrected his bullies. "Ve're just German."

Reuben stood his ground, even though he knew he didn't stand a chance. He was the town outsider, but he was no chicken. Reuben got pulverized so badly that morning, that his refugee parents had no choice but to take him to the overpriced dentist afterwards.

"Well," the orthodontist began, "I'm afraid I have good news and bad news. Which would you like first?"

"Tock, just giff it to us, vill ya?" Mr. Peterson asked, eager to get back to work, so he could get buzzed at the bar afterwards.

"Well, your son did lose a few of his teeth, which somehow have already begun to grow back. The bad news is that his gums are deteriorating and retracting quite a bit."

"He has gingifitis?" his father inquired, not even hearing the part about Reuben's missing teeth being wondrously regenerated.

"No. Whatever this is, it's far more menacing and damaging than gingivitis," the exorbitant dentist confirmed.

Later that night, Reuben wakes up at three in the morning, while his parents are still dead asleep. He's standing in front of the cracked bathroom mirror and is feeling his reborn choppers with his hand. His hijacked teeth had completely grown back, after only one day, and the bottoms were jagged and sharp.

Young Reuben was standing in the doorway again, having one foot in the kitchen and the other in the staircase that led to his bottom dwelling. He just stood there quietly, staring at his mother and hugging the door frame around him. His head was bowed a bit, but his eyes were clearly scoping his maternal guardian.

"Vaht's eating you?" his mother asked, noticing a scowl on her son's face, that clearly revealed his inner unhappiness.

"You could haff helped me," Reuben said, while looking at his mother from out of the corner of his eye, the one that wasn't swelled up anyway. "I saw you. You just stood zere from a tistance and vatched. You could haff tun somezing or called someone."

"Vaht tid you say, you little shit?!" his father asked loudly. "You a vise guy now? If I had effah spoken to my parents zat vay, zay vould haff beaten me senseless."

Insulted and irrational, Gerhard and Helga both met their son at the door. His father angrily picked him up in his arms and hurled Reuben halfway down the stairs. His mother just smiled, and locked the cellar door from the outside. She could tell that her husband was still enraged about Reuben embarrassing him on the baseball field, and decided to calm him down by planting an affectionate smooch on his parched lips.

"Tuz zat make it all bettuh?" she asked.

"Is zat all I get?" Gerhard asked back.

"Not necessarily. Zere might be uhzuh zings up for grabs," she said, chuckling, as she stuck her ass out and wiggled it for him, reaching back and spreading her bare butt cheeks. The Petersons were assholes, and Reuben had haplessly and regretfully gotten acquainted with his mother's anus. He just hadn't scrutinized or penetrated it, the way his father had so many times.

Reuben's health gradually and progressively continued to get worse, eventually being diagnosed with a peculiar strain of the rare blood disorder, *porphyria*. After spending six straight nights lurking and locked away in the cold cellar, Reuben spotted a big rat scampering across the chilled, concrete floor. He instinctively pounced on it without thinking, grabbed it firmly with his clammy hands, and bit into it as if it were a fried chicken leg. Reuben didn't unlatch his jaw from the squealing rodent until he had drained most of its blood. After awhile, the red-haired boy grew to hate his roots, and began to train himself to speak without his German accent. He developed an insatiable craving for sucking and drinking blood, as if it were sweet nectar from a ripe peach. From then on out, Reuben would be homeschooled, self-learned, and as isolated as possible from the public eye.

The years went by slowly but surely, and Reuben's despair became more and more grim. One night, Reuben couldn't sleep. He felt seasick, as if he was suffering from severe motion sickness, yet he had been lying still and idle for hours. He tried to convince himself that he didn't need to be loved, but he was only lying to himself. Though it killed him to admit it, it did bother him that he was unwanted. He contemplated suicide regularly and even scripted detailed plans on how to go about it, but an unseen influence stopped him every time. As miserable and meaningless as his existence was, something inside of him motivated him to live on. He knew that something…or someone…special was waiting for him, he just wasn't prepared for how brief and fleeting his time with her would be.

APRIL 13, 1976
GOOD FRIDAY
RITE OF LUNA

Revelation 22:18-19 (as well as Deuteronomy 4:2 & 12:32) states that a cult is a warped corruption of fundamental Christian doctrine, where elements of the Holy Gospel are added to or subtracted from, to suit and justify a selfish and malevolent agenda (like Mormonism, Islam, or basically any *Christian* minister who asks for generous donations to support his First-Class lifestyle and stock his mansion with assault rifles). By this definition, Satanism is not a *cult*, but a religion. Jeremiah 23:11 tells us that *pastors and prophets are wicked*. Not every prophet is wicked, but just about every minister out there (if not all) is a phony and a prick. As unscrupulous as Satanists are, they are nowhere near as Machiavellian as the so-called *Christian* church. By definition, Christians are *the examples of Christ*, but this is only in theory. If Christ were to return to Earth, in physical form, he would cringe at how many of his alleged followers and spokespeople were shrouded in bigotry, hypocrisy, and shameless cruelty.

Three years ago, in Umatilla County, nestled in the Blue Mountain Range of Northeast Oregon, something very sinister was afoot and about to embark. It was almost the stroke of midnight, and the last of the attendees finished parking at the 64,497-acre ranch. As the celebrants entered the makeshift venue, they were handed free LSD at the door, as well as strong hallucinogens mixed with heavy aphrodisiacs. This was an annual gathering of witches, wizards, and warlocks who worshipped the moon deities and corresponding serpents. Those invited had only been notified of the precise location thirteen hours prior, yet some had traveled there from outside that region. They hadn't gathered there for a country getaway or leisure holiday, but an annual ritual that was unlike any other and unspeakable to anyone who would listen or believe.

This Black Mass was designed to be the ultimate way to ridicule and blaspheme both Christ himself and the faith of Christianity. It is, in many ways, a twisted perversion of the Roman Catholic Mass. The first Black Mass occurred in the 17th Century, initiated by a drug peddling abortionist, named Catherine Deshayes. This month also celebrated the 10th anniversary of *The Church of Satan* being established in San Francisco by carnival showman, Anton LaVey, on April 30, 1966 (aka: *The Witch's Sabbat*). Those attending, as always, were secretly terrified of being chosen, uninformed that a human sacrifice had already been picked and prepared ahead of time. This Black Mass was themed, catering to those sectional Satanists who worshipped the moon and all its phases and forms.

There were 33 members in total, who had been asked to come, not including the hosting Priest and Priestess or other appointed speakers. Those who were already there sat around a 9-ft. pentagram that was salted on the floor. This assembly had gathered at a damp, isolated barn, in the remote country, which had been watered down and smelled of mildew. As usual, most of the patrons were in their mid-teens to late-twenties, but there was always a guest politician, corporate head, or respected clergyman represented. There was one defense attorney, one medical doctor, and even a court judge among this year's participants. Joy and Mathias had traveled there as well, bringing their little slice of Hell to this heinous and blasphemous occasion.

The setting of this infernal shindig was never held in the same place twice, as the weekend activities and festivities were highly immoral and even more illegal. The entrance was heavily guarded with armed security, by a crooked police officer who was equipped with the means to indicate and intervene any potential interference. A male hitchhiker had earlier been abducted and crucified on a crude 9-foot cross, to further mock the good Lord Jesus. Before being dragged onto the stage, the victim had been muzzled and shackled. He kicked and screamed in resistance, though he had been starved for several weeks prior. He had been brutally beaten and mercilessly tortured in the same methods that the Gospel describes Jesus's savage suffering.

"Merry meet," the witches said to one another, greeting those they knew and didn't know, making them feel welcome at this unsettling and unfathomable ceremony.

Mathias was wearing special FX contact lenses, which were solid white with no pupils. They are rigid, uncomfortable, fragile, expensive, and non-disposable, but they definitely brought the effect that he was looking to portray. He and Joy knew how to make an entrance, as all eyes turned toward them as they stepped through the doorway. Mathias and Joy wore long, black dusters that were considerably gothic in design, unlike the rest of their sensuously uniformed coven whom they had temporarily left behind. Everyone there was creepy in their own way, but Mathias and Joy seemed to be the only ones who were eye catching, at least for that moment. The two leaders of *The Golden Veil* were also the only ones at this Black Mass who weren't wearing Druid-like robes and cheap, plastic, animal masks. Mathias despised the Satanic Order, feeling that he should be the lone hierarchy within the organization, but it was time now to represent his Crowleyan family.

The hosting priest stood on the platform, which laid across one end of the barnacle-covered barn, and initiated the Satanic celebration. The High Priest wore a costume that resembled a toad, which had a wide opening at the mouth. He was the disowned stepbrother of *USAR* General, Dr. Michael Aquino. Michael was the highest initiate in *The Church of Satan* the year before, who would abandon LaVey's church near the close of 1975 and found *The Temple of Set*. The thirty-year-old Michael was revered and respected in the *United States Army*, and had rapidly climbed the ladder and breezed through the ranks, in spite of the criminal investigation that proved (but never prosecuted for) the brutal rape of a four-year-old girl. Nikolas Schreck would later convince Zeena LaVey to renounce her father's San Francisco church and join the ranks of Aquino's sect, where she would quickly advance to the esteemed position of *High Priestess*.

"Come forth and shower us with your wicked blessings," he said, holding a small blade in his hand, as if he saw himself as a medieval knight from 5th Century Camelot. "I invoke and conjure thee, by the unholy name of the golden goddess, Isis, who erases light and produces darkness! Protect us from forces both seen and unseen!"

"Isn't he supposed to be using a wand?" Joy whispered in Mathias's left ear, poking fun at the priest's little dagger, while they sat together amongst the rest of the congregants.

"I got your wand right here, bitch," Mathias replied, grabbing his crotch over his khaki slacks, "and it's bigger than that knife." Joy hastily covered her mouth, trying to suppress a snicker.

"Quench our dehydration with the ice that burns!"

The head priest rings a little bell, which is the congregation's cue to stand up.

"Empower and enable us, Lady Isis, also known as, *goddess Diana*! Harm all those who oppose us!" they all shout in unison, as if in a synergy prayer.

It was here that the 33 celebrants disrobed. Everyone undressed and threw their eclectic threads outside of the magic circle, so not to get ruined or stained. A scary woman then entered the Mass, holding a sterling silver chalice with both hands. She stepped off the stage and weaved through the crowd, pouring the gruesome contents over the heads and bodies of the naked parishioners. Even though there was no realistic way for this one cup to hold enough fluid to cover every person in that barn, the chalice seemed to never run dry. What came out of the goblet was sacrificial lamb's blood, mixed with the blood of the human sacrifice and other ingredients that were unspeakable. This process was referred to as a *purification bath*. They allowed this blood to dry and crust on their skin, while the bile priest continued with his offensive sermon and spoke from an obscene pulpit that had hieroglyphic images engraved into the cedar, all of which symbolized either *Isis* or *Baphomet*.

The inside of the barn was decorated with lit blue, green, and black candles that were all made from sacrificial baby fat interweaved with wax. A bell was rung, again by the hosting priest. He held it above his head and rung it hard four times, as he acknowledged the four directions and elements. He then spoke, but this time in a foreign tongue, which sounded like ancient Hebrew. There was a subtle echo, which if you listened closely, sounded as if he had a few different voices spewing from his mouth. Though the words he was saying were clear, it sounded as if he was gargling liquid while he was talking.

"O mighty crystal ball filled with silvery water, I command that the forces of darkness bestow their infernal power upon us, this night. Open wide the Bottomless Pit!" he says, as he holds the athame dagger out in front of him, while throwing out tiny gifts at the crowd. "Rise from the river Styx, and greet us as your brothers and sisters. We favor the just and curse the rotten, given to us the authority by the Voodoo sun god of vengeance, *Shango*, to deem both as we see fit. By *Kun*, and all the other hermaphrodite deities of the Pit, I command the things that I speak to pass. Come forth and answer to your countless names, as you are *Isis* to us, but known as otherwise around the planet. O, hear the names I call. Hilda and Diiwica,"

"Hilda and Diiwica, the white ladies, black earth mothers, and bloodthirsty goddesses of the hunt!" the congregation shouts, as they begin stabbing themselves with what they referred to as *stangs*, but were basically shoplifted thumb tacks.

"Asmodeus, Choronzon, Azazel, Hina, Belial, Akuaba, Amon, Bel, Beelzebub, Lupa, Tython, Megalodon, Feronia, Abaddon, Amaterasu, Samael, Poseidon, Mephisto, Leviathan, Baphomet, Baal, Neptune, Set, Trunko, Astaroth," he continued to name the laundry list of nauseating aliases, while the crowd shouted and repeated each putrid pseudonym as it was said by their deranged and designated priest. "I summon the sentinels of the Bermuda Triangle, to embrace this Eve's chamber and kindle the cold flame of the incarnate divinity, Isis," the atrocious priest said as he continued reading from the *Book of Shadows*.

The sacrilegious priest says something else in a strange dialect, which sounds to be incoherent mumbo jumbo. He then picks up a severed hand from off the fleshy altar, which he is standing behind. As he lifts this stuffed hand in front of his complacent face, the preserved fingertips are somehow ignited with flame, as if the stiff fingers were suddenly candle sticks. The dead hand has a human eye embedded into the center of the palm. The eye is open, as if watching everyone in the wet barn. This morbid hand had been resting on the bare ass of the human altar, which was a nude girl laying flat on her stomach, on a tabletop made of moss-covered red brick. The little bell that the priest had been ringing, sat on the small of her nubile back. When he had removed the *Hand of Glory* from her adolescent butt, she farted in respect, as if she had been holding it in until the moment called for her to release. The bloodcurdling priest frees the eerie hand, and as he removes his hands from it, the disembodied appendage floats on its own will. As this macabre *Hand of Glory* continues to levitate in the air, the High Priest hands a nude boy a pendulum incense holder that had been sitting hidden on the dirty floor.

"Behold, the Heidentor is open," he says, as he continues reading from the Book of Shadows, which lays on the naked girl's upper back. This book contained a number of blasphemous writings, which included their favorite scriptures from the Qur'an (an unholy text that they read from with approbation). As he reads these Islamic whoppers, the blended coven chants in unison.

"O gods and goddesses of the deep Lagoon, manifest thy presence for the achievement of our will?" he dowsed, while the prepubescent altar boy slowly swung the incense back and forth.

Many of the most powerful Satanists across the globe were often Sufi Muslims. Sufis believe that there is no distinction between mankind and God, and that they are their own gods (basic principles of *The Church of Satan*). The Sufi *shaikh* ('saint' or 'teacher') is a master who has power over nature, can both heal and kill with a thought, can communicate directly with Allah, and can compel and control human hearts. This is what they believe. Sufis are also known to release beast-like demons (called *jinn* or *djinn*) to harm those who debate or rebel (*infidels*). Allah has no *likeness* and no divine Son. Their prophet, Muhammad, was infamous for his fondness for murder and pedophilia. So, as you can see, Islam is a Satanist's best friend, as the two theologies are ridiculously similar. On a side note, Muslims say they accept the Judeo-Christian Gospel, but believe that it was tampered with, and therefore say that it's based on the works of man and not God. More Christians ponder this troubling thought every day, as more seminary *scholars* (which aren't experts at anything but pomposity and enmity) insist on publishing a different so-called Biblical *interpretation* or *translation* for every day of the month.

"The cold flame consumes me," says the brainwashed altar boy, as he hands the charcoal brazier back to the High Priest after he had swung it back and forth six times.

"The cold flame consumes me," the High Priest says back, as he places the incense pendulum back on the filthy floor. "Tonight, we drink to honor our true nature," he says as he sips from the repugnant chalice. He then passes it to his altar boy, who sips it and then holds it up above his young head.

"The joy of Hathor is with me," the altar boy says, before returning it to the hands of the middle-aged High

Priest. "Hathor, the horned moon goddess who wears a cobra headdress, who carries the Eye of Ra, plays the tambourine, and has the features and characteristics of a cow! The joy of Hathor is with me!"

"Joy is with me," Mathias leans over and whispers in Joy's ear, making her smile as he holds her hand in his. Joy barely suppresses her laugh this time, by curling her lips inward and biting down, as to keep her mouth tightly shut.

"The joy is in the flesh," the High Priest adds, holding up the black-handled blade. "By the floods of Atlantis, I call forth Lady Isis and all of her aliases and minions." He turns his body. "From the South, the infernal Shakti, I summon thee," he says as he points the blade in that direction with an outstretched arm in front of him. "From the East, bringer of nausea and disease, deception and destruction, the sphinx twins, Pasht and Bast, I bid thee welcome! From the North, the goddess of pain and harm, Skadi, I summon thee and bid thee welcome." He turns again, this time facing the crowd. "From the West, raging serpent of the watery Abyss, the repulsive Leviathan, I summon thee and bid thee welcome. Hail, Kali Ma, the black mother of torture, torment, and terror! You control the weather by braiding your hair!" the priest shouts.

A bell is rung by the nameless woman who distributed the cleansing blood bath. This High Priestess steps in front of the High Priest and speaks, as she raises her arms up at her sides, blatantly mocking the way Jesus' arms were while hanging on the cross.

"Yemaya, goddess of the seas, unto thee is power and dominion. Let our Left Hand visions be manifested and enduring, for we are the children of earthly delights. Cybele, goddess of the beasts of the moon! Give us thy blessing!" she says as she turns to face the South. "Full moon goddess, Allat!" she says, turning to face the East, with her back against the crowd. "Bid us thy favor! Scatha, the shadowy one who strikes fear, defecate on us, your followers." She then points the athame dagger at the attendees. "Soma, Indian moon god of immortality, bestow to us your treasures." She turns and walks back to her High Priest, returning the blade to him, which he then responds by bowing his head in respect and gratitude. The athame dagger has a message, in a strange alphabet, engraved on the double-sided blade.

He lifts the knife up above his head, holding it horizontally with a hand at either end. His assisting Priestess then spreads the ass cheeks of the girl laying on the altar, so he can stick the handle end of the dagger up the young lady's butthole. The knife is now sticking straight out of her delectable, teenage bum.

"Let not your wrath be extinguished or stifled. O Isis, goddess of lightning, guardian of the Left Hand Path, and monster of the river Styx, present your malignant power. Purify and consecrate this altar and this Mass through the bite of frost. Strike down our adversaries!

Let those cower in terror, formed or formless, who would dare afflict the coldhearted. Let them drown for eternity in the Lake of Liquid Nitrogen. Artemis, restore yourself to power and reveal your exalted radiance, unleashing your fury and vengeance with your silver bow and, *Alani*, your silver hound. Harrow your emergence, which engulfs you. This we command, in the name of our Lady Moon, Shing-Moo. Her mercies flourish into sustenance will. We will prevail!"

"Hail Nehellania, dark moon of the Nether realm! Samen!" The congregation repeats this last word six times. "Hail Tlazolteotl, goddess of filthy bats, snakes, and black witchcraft! Samen!" The congregation once again repeats this word six times. The propolos (or *attendant who leads*) rings the bell yet again.

"As Hecate reigns, so shall her frozen vessels," he says, as he vehemently flicks the knife, making it jiggle and vibrate in the girl's tight anus. "Give us life everlasting on this earth, bringing tidal waves to only those who oppose us. Grant us a world without end, and end those who rebuke or persecute us." He primitively yanks out the knife and brings the handle part up to his mouth, where he then proceeds to suck on the phallic object that is soaked with the girl's anal secretions.

Organ music begins to play in the background, though there is no visible sign of any such instrument. This music fails to overpower or undermine the voices of the High Priest and Priestess, who both have the undeserved admiration of the indoctrinated and misguided followers. The High Priest crosses his arms over his chest and then steps off the polluted pulpit. The High Priestess takes over and positions herself behind the altar, where he had stood. She removes the chalice from the human altar's armpit and brings it up to hold against her bosom. As the priestess holds this diseased goblet with her right hand, she shoves her left hand into the young girl's vagina, aggressively fingering and fisting her. The cold-hearted priestess continues to sexually violate the adolescent girl until her pussy becomes saturated with her underdeveloped juices. Once this occurs, the priestess pulls her wet hand out and cleans it off by wiping it all over the rim of the chalice. The dark priestess hands the smeared cup of blood to the High Priest, who rejoins her back on stage and hands her the filthy dagger. The *Hand of Glory* is still hovering feet above the human altar.

"Set free the lust and temptation that burns within you," the High Priestess says, as she holds the athame dagger out in front of her bosom. "Come forth, monsters of the great storm, and make thy presence known. Join us in celebrating our hedonistic endeavors. Send forth thy venomous vermin upon us, that we may please your infernal majesty with our wicked delights. To the house of harlots, unashamed of the animals that God designed us to be. To all the pleasures of the night, we revel. The life of Lady Isis consumes me," she says as she sips from the chalice, which the hosting priest holds up for her to drink from. She hands it to the altar boy who then pisses in it and hands it back to her. "The joy of the flesh is eternal," she reads from the book, and then sips from the chalice that appears to be bottomless. She walks around the human altar so that she now stands in front of it and not behind it. "Let the six symbols of the Beast lurketh as we await your release. Through the nourishment of our sacrifice, let the angels cringe in terror. Let this sacrament fill the void of night, and let its lust illuminate its darkness, which leadeth to the Left Hand Path. Coyolxauhqui!"

The coven repeats this deplorable word of extreme silliness, following it with, "Hail Semele!"

The eerie bell is rung again. The High Priest faces his High Priestess, while they hold the chalice between them. They speak together in a foreign tongue, as a myriad of different voices flow from their mouths. They then refill the chalice with their own blood and bodily functions (spit, piss, and sperm) and mix it with a crimson red wine. "Amidst the rampage of our orgy, staggers the Devil herself. In the musky night, with yummy brains, passion shall take hold into writhing and twisting bodies. The great Wahini-Ahi, the original woman and creator of this world, shall preside over all," the priest and priestess say simultaneously together, as if their minds are tuned in to the same wavelength.

She turns to the audience. "As evil reigns, may all your sadistic desires be fulfilled. We shall have everlasting life and a world without end."

A shirtless man comes up on the pulpit, as the High Priest and Priestess temporarily step off. He has open scars on his cheeks that are made to look like gills, while his face and head are completely bald. He has surgically-implanted horns attached to his skull that push out from his forehead. He picks up the dagger and loudly addresses the crowd, as if they were severely hard of hearing.

"Before the mighty prince of darkness and the dreaded piranha of the Pit, and before this company infernal, we proclaim that Aphrodite, otherwise known as, *Lady of the Wild Things*, and *Patroness of Prostitutes*, rules the earth! We ratify and renew our pledge to glorify her without reservation, desiring in return her manifold assistance in successful completion of our endeavors and the fulfillment of our lusts. O friend and companion of the night, thou who delights in the brains of dogs, who seeks to torment and terrorize; and who longs for the spilt blood of the honorable and noble. Lord of the moon, look favorably upon our bodies of water, which we prepare now in thy many infernal names." He sets down the blade and picks up the chalice. "I drink from this vile goblet, to beat the power of death," he says as he sips from the cup. "O honored brother of darkness, drink from this chalice and never die." He hands it to the altar boy, who holds it over his head, raising it with pride, as if making a toast.

"To the annihilation of all fanatics, enslaved to spiritual myth and morality. Destroy the vile hypocrites, who are the rabid disease of mankind and a bane on all civility. To this, I issue my own oath that these mad dogs will be obliterated. Long live Ra, Isis, and the shape-shifters of the Great Night, *Morrigan* and *Frigga*!" the choir boy shouts, as he hands it back to the horned fish-man.

"Joy to the flesh forever!" the freakish man exclaims, as his dark presence loomed over the parishioners. He bends over to touch his feet, and as he does, the congregation sees a subdermal implant that resembles a fin on his naked back. This kind of surgery was hidden from most of the world and only revealed to those who were astronomically rich. "From the tips of our toes to the tops of our scalps, let us celebrate our supreme bodies! Joy to the flesh forever!"

"Your flesh gives me joy, Joy," Mathias whispered half-jokingly to her, trying to make Joy laugh again, while also attempting to turn her on at the same time.

"Do what thou wilt!" says the blended coven in unison. "The only real sin is self-denial!"

"Behold the prince of sea serpents, as I point this athame to the four directions and elements of the earth. I have become a monstrous machine of obliteration, festering on body fragments of those who would detain or malign me. Black shapes of ooze shall rise from the darkest pits of the Great Bay, and vomit forth superiority upon their puny minds. I call for the messengers of doom to slash with grim delight, upon the victims I have chosen. Torment with agony, any who betray us, as signals of warning to those who oppose us. O great brothers and sisters of the deep night, I call upon the great barracuda, *Abaddon*, to dwelleth in the Kraken's vein and smite those who scorn us. Come, o night, which we have made our home, and sustain us in your majesty. Rip out the tongues and seal the mouths of our enemies. Slaughter the frail and the weak, who pollute our existence and mock our authority. Pierce their lungs with the electric stings of eels, o Dione! Cast their substance into the dismal void, o mighty Dagon," the genetically-modified man said, before turning the pulpit back over to the hosting priest. His concubine priestess again joins him on stage, now holding a small bell in each hand.

"O infernal majesty, throw them into the Pit evermore to suffer perpetual anguish. Bring thy hurricane upon them, o rulers of the slimy underworld, that they may know the extent of thy anger. Call forth thy legions to witness what they do in thy name. Send forth thy messengers to proclaim this dirty deed, and call forth the great Lochness to step forth from the iron gates of the bottomless sinkhole. Stand tall and crush the pitiful infidel with your cloven hooves. Let loose the hounds of Hell to rip flesh and crush bone. Smite them anew, o lord of the cold flame, that their gods and goddesses, priests and prophets, may cower before thee in fear, trembling and suffocating before themselves, in respect of thy power. Send a mighty tornado to crash down the majestic gates of their heavens and nirvanas."

She rings the left bell, and then the High Priest continues with his obnoxious and offensive rant.

"Banish into nothingness, the vile and abhorrent pretenders to the splendor of the Full Moon goddess, *Maia*. Return to the void of thy empty heavens. For the lord, Astarte, who reigns over Jahi the Whore and all the prostitutes and adulteresses, brings others to perish under his mighty cloven feet. Coyolxauhqui!"

The blended coven repeats this ridiculous word.

"Hail Rhea! Youth of Sparta!"

Again, this mixed coven repeats this blasphemy that they have become all too familiar and comfortable with. She rings the bell in her right hand.

"I place my darkest blessings upon this diabolical brethren, who walk the way of the cold flame." He folds his hands together and bows his head, as if in prayer. "The essence of the Satanist is pure vengeance, thus we proceed ever forward. So, my Luciferian comrades, indulge, innovate, and celebrate the unique life that is your precious treasure. Do what thou wilt, and go forth filling your days with ecstasy and malice unending. As High Priest of this melting pot of covens and magus of

The Black Order, I place my benediction upon you, as your lives are filled with triumphs unbounded." The repugnant pope moves his left hand as if making the sign of the cross, but with his hand in the sign of the horns. "As you exist in the eternal now, live in exquisite greed and lust. So mote it be!" He crosses his arms over his chest, still making the sign of the horns, now with both hands. "Hail the threefold goddess, full of might! Maiden, Mother, and the Crone delight! Our allegiance is with thee! So mote it be!"

"Our allegiance is with thee! So mote it be!" the combined coven repeats in unison, without question or hesitation, as the High Priestess changes into a costume in front of everyone.

"Cursed are the god adorers of false piety, and cursed are the worshippers of the peaceful Nazarene. Unholy Diana, bringer of enlightenment, lend us thy power at this midnight hour. The Catholic Church depicts Mary with the lunar crown, which was wrongfully stolen from your possession. You are the witch with cones of power! Coyolxauhqui!"

The cumulation of covens repeats this stupid word one final time, before the Satanists got up one by one, from the salt-drawn, 9-foot pentagram that they had been sitting in, and formed a single line to wait for their turn to partake of the unholy eucharist. The High Priestess is now wearing a costume that resembles an octopus, which has only one opening...which is at her buttocks. The fake tentacles are shortened in length, as to not prevent access to her ass. She is completely nude underneath the costume.

"One day, I'm going to be the High Priest of this Order," Mathias whispered into Joy's ear. "The day will come when I won't have to bow to anyone, god or man." Joy just smiled at him, not saying anything in either agreement or argument. "When I'm in charge of everything, I won't be an anonymous *High Priest* either. Everyone will know my name," he added, before they got up to get in line, to participate in the blasphemous Communion.

The repulsive alchemist ejaculated his sperm into the chalice, by an effective combination of self-masturbation and from the altar boy pleasing him with oral copulation. They then further laced the concoction by spitting and pissing in the contaminated goblet, stirring and mixing the detestable brew with a black candle stick. The head priest then offered the revolting libations from the profane cup, after asking the moon goddess, Isis, to bless over the Unholy Sacrament. The Black Communion was consumed from the plagued chalice, which was still refilling itself as quickly as it was emptied. As the congregants took turns holding the cup, they saw that the surface of the mixture showed a reflection of a crescent moon accompanied by a small star (the *Islam* symbol). By sipping from this goblet mixture, they firmly believed that it would give them ultimate and infinite power.

As the members were served one at a time, they held out their hands or open mouth to receive some of the abominable contents. Once each congregant partook of their portion and had their share of the distorted version of the eucharist, they handed the cup back to the horned man. They then paid their respects to the two elders, depending on what gender they were. The females planted a tongue-kiss on the mouth of the High Priest, who was dressed like a toad. If the parishioner was a male, he used his tongue to rim the dirty anus of the High Priestess, who turned around and spread her ass cheeks for them to lick.

"As the cup is to the goddess," the High Priestess spoke, after removing her farcical costume and having it taken away by the young altar boy.

"So the athame is to the god," the High Priest contributed.

"And conjoined, they bring blessedness," the crowd said in unison.

"Bless this bread of human flesh and this potion of bodily functions, bestowing upon us all the wicked desires of our cold hearts," the hosting priest added. He then paused and momentarily departed from the evening's objective, as if something had just come over him that he felt necessary to urgently address in the midst of this annual ceremony. "I am led by the darkness to tell someone here, a personalized message from beyond. You will soon find and achieve great euphoria in a young girl. She will be one of immense beauty, but who possesses a shattered heart that feels uninhibited passion, undying love, and animalistic rage. If you pursue her relentlessly and stay the course in spite her resistance, she will bring you ecstasy that can't be defined in any language. She will look, on the surface, to be a vulnerable kitten, while concealing a dark secret that reveals something beastly and monstrous."

Whether than appreciate his privileged position, Mathias (blessed with a coven of young women who were blindly devoted to him) secretly wished that the priest's foretelling prophecy would be intended for (and directed at) him. Not only was he beyond greedy and ungrateful, but Mathias was the epitome of hypocrisy, as he wished horrible death on his fellow cozeners, whom he was clearly jealous of. He hated and envied those in authority and power, even though he was cut from the same cloth and had no legitimate reason to complain. Once everyone in the barn had a drink from the chalice, the floor was open for them to have more. The High Priestess rolled out a small cauldron, which contained bits and pieces of the carved-up human sacrifice.

The illegal (and primarily undisclosed) narcotics that the cannibals had swallowed in the beginning of the ritual (which they chased down with flavored liquor) had really kicked in by this point. As dark as it was in this desecrated barn, many of the congregants were seeing the colors of the rainbow. Worries were forgotten, inhibitions were dropped, and any leftover repression was replaced with rage, rebellion, and revolution. The only ones who were immune to this acid trip were those who had declined partaking in the preparation-drug-use or the unholy eucharist, which those responsible for securing and administering the event were allowed to do. The High Priest and Priestess led the congregation in reciting the *Lord's Prayer* backwards, to further blaspheme the immaculate Lord Jesus.

"I bid thee rise and give the sign of the horns," the hosting priest said, just before the witches and warlocks stood up and raised their left hands. "O mighty Isis, open wide the gates of the Abyss and make them serve you. Govern those who govern. Cast down those who fall. Reward those who increase and succeed, and destroy the poor and the pathetic. Thank you for the ancient powers of the East and the South! Thank you for your presence and the blessings of your fair realms. We are the partakers of your undefiled wisdom. We bid you hail and farewell. Forget ye not what was, and is to be. Flesh without sin. World without end. Coyolxauhqui!"

The intoxicated crowd once again repeats this dimwitted word that the Satanic religion held in such high regard. Mathias and Joy were stoned along with the rest of their peers, and had become considerably dazed and bemused. They had temporarily lost all sense of judgment and control, and just went along with what everyone else was saying and doing around them.

"Hail Demeter!" the nameless High Priestess yells, followed by the condensed congregation repeating her foolish words.

She rings a bell six times, while facing each of the four directions. The High Priest reaches into a rune bag, pulling out a healthy handful of *I Ching* coins, and throws them violently out into the crowd, as if trying to pelt the audience in the face with the innocuous divination devices. The Mass ends with *sex magick*, after a sloppy feast of cakes and wine. Every sexual perversion and abomination is performed and indulged.

"Mescalito is calling!" one witch yells, as she straddles over a guy's mouth to relieve herself of piss and vinegar, pulling up on the top of her crotch to better aim her golden stream.

"Bendis, the Greek goddess of orgies, is here to inspire our indulgence!" another belted out.

Bestiality, pedophilia, necrophilia, and sex with demons were all experimented and engaged. As a necessary precaution for intercourse with the revolting incubi, the female members had to coat the inside of their pussies with salt, to prepare for the gelid demon-sperm. The incubi's erection pointed down instead of up. The barn permeated with the scent of fish, from all the naked female genitalia that hadn't been washed in thirteen days. This degenerate orgy is followed by a group dance around the salt-drawn, nine-foot pentagram.

"Nature is the gown the goddess wears, and we dance to express her majesty. Hail Melusine!" the High Priestess shouts out.

Eerie Classical music plays once again, from no visible or material source. The bats in the belfry roar and cheer like rabid beasts, using many voices from the various demons that possess each of them. Praises are loudly offered to the Egyptian fertility god, Osiris, who is also known as, *the god of transformation.*

The leftover human remains were incinerated and then buried in wet cement. Some of the smaller bones were salvaged for either the purpose of making jewelry or to be used as tools in future rituals. Before the remains are disposed of, the lips of the human sacrifice were sealed and hot wax was poured onto the eyes, in barbaric attempts to keep the victim from having the pleasure and honor of spending eternity in Heaven.

The climax to Dawn's riveting story resumes three years after the unsettling, '76 flashback you just read…

They say that *all good things must come to an end*, and Dawn, despite her flaws, is certainly that. It has been an honor for me to write Dawn's story, and though this will be the final book, I know she will always be with me and continue to be a part of who I am. I hope you, my appreciated readership, feel the same way. If not, I believe you just might, once you have finished reading this third novel.

Thank you for your time and support, and for welcoming Dawn into your life and your world.

MARCH 24, 1979

Cheri threw a *Moon Pie* wrapper out the window, as she and Wolf continued cruising down the endless highway, with the *Shen* medallion bouncing and dangling off the rear-view mirror. The sun-god relic is flapping around to the semi-loud music playing on Cheri's *Dodge* Van radio. Carly Simon's, *Nobody Does It Better*, the theme to the James Bond film, *The Spy Who Loved Me*, is playing. Wolf is laying down in the back, covering his face with his arms, secretly fearful that his new guardian may have lost it. Cheri had been talking and singing to herself, as well as falling into spells where her eyes rolled back into her head and she laughed for no reason.

"What's happening, Cheri? I don't know, foxy? What's happening with you, chica?" she asked and answered herself. "How's life treating you? Has it been a bowl of cherries?" she asked herself, bursting out laughing while crying simultaneously.

Even though Cheri still had Wolf's company and companionship, his amazing friendship wasn't enough. To keep from going crazy, Cheri acted like the Mad Hatter (in *Disney's* 1951 animated feature) by monopolizing the conversation with herself. She had said her goodbyes to reality, not knowing how to cope with how she felt about Dawn and no longer having her in her possession. Cheri was part succubus, and was neither designed or prepared to feel these bewitching emotions of love. It was unnatural and broke every rule in the Cambion handbook. Neither Cheri or Dawn should have been surprised with the turn of events, as they were both downbeat souls who suffered from Cherophobia (which is the belief that as soon as one finds happiness, something bad will occur as direct punishment).

It was Dawn's 20th birthday today, and Cheri hated having to spend it without her puppy love. Little did she know that Dawn was hurting much more than she was, as Dawn was in a Hell of a different sort, being held by real monsters, and because of Joy's curse, she had no strength to save herself. *She's the One*, by The Ramones, came on her Van's stereo, only adding insult to injury. The radio stations seemed to have it out for her, as this song was followed by George Harrison's, *What is Life*, followed by Donna Summer's, *Love To Love You Baby*. Whatever station she turned it to made no difference, as every dial played similar tunes. It was as if her Van was trying to live up to it's paint job, by playing only Blues. Cheri came close to ripping her radio out and tossing that out the window too, but she knew she would regret it if she did. Music was literally the only thing, at this point, that kept her from blowing her brains out. Besides, any music was better than dismal silence.

Wolf was just as sad without and worried about Dawn, as Cheri was, but he seemed to be alone in his sanity. He was literally the only one in the troop who was keeping it together. Wolf knew that Cheri had no clue where they were going, but hoped that maybe her precarious state of mind might work for them and somehow change their luck. Cheri had finally given up on fighting the radio, and had settled on one station. Chicago's, *If You Leave Me Now*, began playing. As soon as Cheri recognized what song it was, she let out a closed-mouth growl, which started soft and subtle but escalated in volume. Wolf heard her and knew she was about to blow her top, so out of anticipation, he dug his huge claws into the carpeted floor of the Van. Cheri banged her forehead against the steering wheel, as if she were attempting to give herself a concussion. Wolf was wise to grab onto the floor and secure himself the way he had, because not even a minute later, she drove over a huge pothole that had been ignored and untended in the middle of the highway. The *Dodge* Van managed to make it over safely, but not without repercussions. Not only did it flatten one of their tires, but Cheri paid for not being buckled up.

"Son of a bitch!" she screamed, as her butt came off the seat and the top of her head hit the roof of her Van. Wolf was okay, thankful that he had shown better intuition than she did, at least in that moment. Cheri swerved off and parked alongside the road, to gather herself and take a breather. "Wolf," she said, with her eyes closed and her head down. "After we get our Dawn back…remind me to find out where these goddamn radio stations are. I'd like to pay them a visit, and personally thank them for their choice in music today," she said, half-serious and half-caustic. Cheri's cerebral cauldron was boiling over, and she felt herself coming to the brink of blowing her psychological lid, when she finally turned and looked at Wolf. Seeing the frightened expression on his face, her steamed temper quickly cooled, realizing how her outburst had affected him. "I'm so sorry," she told him, stroking the top of his head and scratching under his lower jaw. "I'm sorry, Wolf."

Her eyes watered, as she saw the daunted light in his yellow eyes. She had caused him to feel apprehensive around her, when she was the one who was supposed to make him feel safe. Cheri snapped out of her tantrum and apologized to Wolf a third time for her reckless temper, which in turn, endangered him unintentionally.

While Wolf waits inside, Cheri repairs the partially deflated tire by touching it with her infernal hand, instinctively discovering one of the few benefits of being fifty-percent demon. Not only is she able to magically call upon the winds to fill the tire to where it needs to be, but she is able to plug and seal the hole by raising the temperature in her hand to an inhuman degree. Her hand got so hot that it was the equivalent of a butane torch, just without the actual flame.

"Let's see Arianrhod of Wales do that," Cheri said, scoffing at the nonsense she had learned about witchcraft. "Dark goddess of the moon, my ass. Let's see her silver-wheel bullshit do this. I don't need a false deity from the *Aurora Borealis* to help me carry Wolf and I back to my starry counterpart. All I need is love."

As Cheri got back into the Van, she gave Wolf a warm hug, held him tight and close for a few quality moments, and then got them back on the road. Wolf came up and sat in what used to be Dawn's seat, while the song, *Hard To Say I'm Sorry*, played. Cheri actually began to sing along to this *Chicago* song, as it played melodically through her speakers. As they drove down the freeway, Cheri began to notice that several of the *Exit* signs had phrases on them instead of proper nouns. The signs were telling her to turn back, give up, and let Dawn go. The signs weren't really saying these things, but in Cheri's mind…they were. Whenever she saw this, she immediately shook her head and forcibly blinked her eyes, trying to push out the bad thoughts. She kept this quietly to herself, not wanting to scare Wolf any more than she regretfully already had.

Meanwhile, Dawn is fantasizing about when she was still over-the-moon happy. She opens her blue eyes, still in the dream, bright eyed and bushy tailed. Cheri is spooning her from behind, while they're both naked on the bed. Wolf is licking Dawn's nose, trying to wake her up.

Suddenly, Dawn is looking at herself, as she hovers over her own body. The scene changes to the venue parking lot, when Dawn pushes Cheri away and abandons Wolf. Dawn wakes up again, but this time for real. Her body is covered in perspiration, and she's panting heavily with quick, short breaths. Her broken heart is beating a mile a minute, her head is aching and weighted, and she's locked away in a cell that's much worse than what she once knew at the Virginian mental ward. The main difference was that…here…she had no freedom or special privileges. She looked like she had been messed up and pounded pretty bad, along with bite marks on her neck and inner thighs. Dawn had been here for three months, and had been doped up each and every day against her will. Her traffickers sedated her with heavy drugs before they would brutalize and sodomize her.

Dawn's out cold again, sprawled out on the colder floor. As she slept under the influence, she dreamt again, this time finding herself kneeling at a brook. She drank furiously from the small stream and noticed her reflection amidst all the ripples in the water. Her ears had grown long and pointed, looking stretched and sticking straight up through her shimmering hair. Her entire body was gleaming with an outline of bright, pink light. She glowed, as if she had just been dangerously exposed to nuclear radiation. She felt powerful and unstoppable, until she looked around her and realized that she was alone. Wolf wasn't there, he was absent, and it was her fault. It was her fault.

"Wolf?" she cried, distressed and disoriented. "Wolf?! Where are you? I'm sorry! I'm so sorry!" As she sobbed desperately and frantically for her dear friend, her distraught nightmare wasn't quite done with her yet.

Dawn was visited by a devilish dwarf, who invaded her dreams against her will. He was nothing like *Imp*, the midget she had briefly encountered at the carnival. This dwarf was a whole other creature altogether and was there for an entirely different reason. His head was in the shape of a crescent moon, and he was colored red from head to toe.

"Venez en France," he told her, speaking in a dialect that was foreign to her.

"I don't understand?" she replied, spooked by his wickedly-wide grin and shark-like teeth. Even though Dawn was dreaming and he was smiling, this creature felt palpable and menacing.

When she came out of her dream state, she returned to feeling sick and weak instead of strong and superhuman. She looked at her hair, holding the ends in her hands. Before her very eyes, her hair turned colors. In one moment, her locks were solid white, while in the next, her hair retained its beautiful brown with only streaks of white. Dawn was fully awake now, but obviously still in her nightmare. She began tugging on her hair, pulling it out. This led to her smacking the sides of her head with her clenched fists, crying and screaming, as her eyes widened and rolled into the back of her head. It took her less than a minute to put together that she had acted out her dream, when she saw the frightened faces on the five other girls who were sharing her cell. Dawn spotted them huddling together in the corner, all shaking like a leaf, while they stared back at her in utter fear and unspeakable horror.

Dawn was drenched in her own perspiration, her eyes were saturated with tears, and her heart was racing and beating like a steel drum. Adrenaline pulsed through her veins and she feverishly felt the need to kill, but her will power was much stronger than her dark intent.

"Is she going to hurt us?" Julie asked out loud, feeling endangered by Dawn's clear signs of mental illness, not knowing if she was a fellow victim or a harmful plant.

"Absolutely," Teri answered, who was a compulsive (and impulsive) liar.

Dawn, of course, was no threat to anyone, thanks to the trick flask that was maliciously plagued with personalized curses from Joy and Mathias. It hurt for Dawn to inhale, but she had to breathe in deep due to being out of breath. Her heart was still pounding as if there was no tomorrow, while her elbows trembled violently as she tried her best to hold herself up. Dawn missed Cheri terribly, but felt particularly alone without Wolf. They had built such a bond between them that could only be defined as one soul split into two bodies. Wolf was a part of her, and being apart from him was its own death.

There was nowhere for her to lurk, which killed her because Dawn wanted nothing more than to ambush and annihilate her perpetrators. It also bothered her that she wasn't able to strike down Richard Ramirez, as her intuition told her that his name would become a cancer on mankind. That ship, to her regret, had sailed. Richard was gone, never to be seen again by her. He, much like Zeena, had brought her on board just to leave her stranded. Dawn was trying to dog paddle on her own, but her arms and legs were getting tired. The harder she fought to persevere, the more seasick she became. Dawn was a castaway on an island that she had built herself.

Because it had been so long since Dawn killed anyone or left any clues to her current whereabouts, Agent Shelling had pretty much hung up the towel. He didn't have much of a choice, since his superiors had lost any interest in keeping the case open. They had given up faith on Shelling's ability to find her and he couldn't really blame them. Dawn's elusive methods had wiped out his self-confidence, and his hatred for her had quite honestly exhausted his energy. She had evaded him at every turn, and none of his detective skills or government resources appeared to be making a difference. He had finally met his match, and nothing he could do would change the fact that she had beaten him.

Shelling found himself sitting in the middle of nowhere, taking in the glory and majesty of the great outdoors. This was what his intention was anyhow, but the reality was, he didn't get it. He had long wondered about the obsession that so many proud Americans shared about nature. He had even set up a tent, tried his hand at fishing, and drank a suitcase of *Genuine Draft* by a bonfire. Yet, no matter how hard he tried to get bit by the camping bug, it only confused and puzzled him further on how so many women adored this shitty lifestyle. Even after coating himself in aerosol spray, he was eaten alive by all the different species and breeds of insects. They ruthlessly swarmed around him, ignoring the ineffective deterrent he had wasted money on. If the sun wasn't blazing only on him, trying to give him carcinoma, it was showering failure. However, when it rained, it either poured like an *Old Testament* plague, or it drizzled just enough to be annoying but unrefreshing.

"You know what? Fuck this. Fuck this! I don't need this shit," he said aloud to himself, as he threw the empty *Coors* bottle at the falling sunset. "Fuck the *FBI*! Fuck my dead nephew! Fuck Dawn Moon! Fuck every vicious bitch who got her kicks from ripping my heart out! And fuck my life! Fuck it! Fuck this!" he shouted, as he struggled to get on his feet, only to lose his balance half way up and collapse on the ground beneath him.

APRIL 8, 1979
PALM SUNDAY

"God blesses those who work for peace. These, my friends, are the true children of God," the priest said, quoting Matthew 5:9. By *peace*, the priest covertly meant *piece*…as in *piece of ass*…taking notice of the four eye-catching, young women visiting his fraudulent Mass.

Joy, Maria, Bonnie and Emily are sitting in a restored Catholic church that would have easily impressed the most hardened agnostic. The religious building had cathedral interior, antique pews, crimson-colored carpet, and majestic stained-glass windows that looked like they were donated by the Vatican itself. While keeping busy not listening to the priest, the witches are fiddling with the palms. When I say *palms*, I'm not referring to their hands, but the green and bendable bamboo that were handed out to everyone attending Mass. They notice that everyone is playing with them and shaping them into crosses.

"You need to make your crucifix before the palms dry out," one elderly patron said, taking notice that the girls were idly holding them and therefore not respecting the tradition.

Joy glanced at her three peers, grinned wickedly, and came up with the blasphemous idea of making their palms into an ankh instead. "Let's fuck with this old hag," Joy suggested in a whisper. "What do you say, girls? Let's have some fun with this."

Maria fondled the palm and fidgeted in her seat, as she grew progressively pissed with her bamboo splitting on the ends, which made it significantly difficult to manipulate and mold it. Frustrated, she throws hers on the ground, immediately getting a hostile reaction from the rest of the congregation.

"Those palms are blessed, young lady!" one man called out, as if he could mysteriously hear the damaged palms hit the floor. "You don't throw blessed palms away, you heretic! You burn them, so that the ashes return to Heaven!"

Joy throws her head back and cackles loudly, while her equally amused girlfriends cover their mouths and make an earnest effort not to burst out laughing. They find it silly that these palms are viewed as sacred, much in the same vein that most Americans regard their nation's flag, which they also find to be quite preposterous. It's here, at this moment, that the prized queen of deceit comes out of her pleasant flashback.

Joy is sitting in the seat next to her glorified religious guru. She and Mathias were moving down the highway in a black hearse that they had ripped off. Their coven was dead and murdered, Joy having brutally butchered them, using knives and guns instead of her infernal *Arae* powers. Joy had left sole survivor, Emily Bryant, with the hope that this abominable apostle could convince the pragmatic authorities that Dawn had been the culprit. This, however, made little to no sense, considering that Dawn's signature never came in bullets or blades. Agent Shelling was not fooled by Emily, but interrogated her only to extract a series of whoppers from her lying lips. He knew better, and wasn't gullible enough to fall for someone who plainly lacked credibility. That was all over with now, freeing Joy and Mathias to conquer the world as a diabolical duo instead of a complicated coven. The Moving Sidewalks song, *Crimson Witch*, plays over the installed radio, as Joy and Mathias both bob their heads to the psychedelic tune.

Cheri is clothed in a head scarf, wrap dress, and platform boots. She drives behind a car, which has rear tags that say, *Virginia is for Lovers*. She notices these license plates while ELO's version of The Move's 1972 song, *Do Ya*, plays over her radio. She impulsively cranks up the volume to try and drown out her distressing thoughts with the loud music, but then quickly turns it back down, out of concern for Wolf's ear drums. She pulls her Van up to a popular restaurant and once she parks, she grabs her steering wheel with both hands and tries to talk herself through the flood of chaos in her head. She had turned the Van around several times, not able to decide on or commit to one direction. There is a forked stick, which Cheri had tied to the hood, with rope that reached around the entire front of the vehicle. This made her Van look corny rather than groovy, but she believed that the wooden hood ornament would magically guide them in the right direction. She also trusted in something that could only be described as an inner compass leading her on where to go, which would also prove to be significantly disappointing.

"I have no idea where we're going. I suddenly wish I had been born an Indian, like Dawn, but…" Cheri stopped the pessimism, noticing that her despondent energy was negatively affecting Wolf. "We will emerge victorious," she said aloud, in an effort to both console Wolf and convince herself, through positive thinking and attitude. "But first we must refuel." Wolf was just as hungry as she was, so he had no complaints about her spontaneous decision to stop.

Cheri orders a *Watergate Salad* and a tall glass of tap water, while Wolf waits in the Van with the windows rolled down. She battles her inner demons of doubt and inadequacy, while struggling to keep her strength. Her bones, joints, and lower back were in sheer agony. Being separated from Dawn had taken a real toll on her health, but not nearly as much as it had on her heart. Cheri more than missed her, and *love* wasn't a big enough word. She needed Dawn and all that this codependency entailed. She hated herself for having used her, but was determined to make things right, even if it meant giving her own life to save hers. She regretted ever playing her, and now found herself in a game that she should have known she couldn't win.

As Wolf looks out of the passenger window, that Cheri had thoughtfully left rolled down for him, he spots a passing couple who aren't nearly as courteous. They are quarreling belligerently, as they walk briskly to his brand-new car.

"I can love Jesus, and not want kids, asshole! Just because I don't drool over the rancorous ritual of marriage, like you do, doesn't make me an antichrist. What kind of a name is *Hollis*, anyway? Sounds pretty gay to me," Brooke asked her toxic boyfriend, who somehow managed to be a highly respected member of their community. Not only was he a man of influence and authority, but he had the police department in his privileged pocket.

"You're aching for a breaking, Brooke," the two-faced minister threatened, as he struggled to keep up with his much younger, ravishing playmate.

He was panting and out of breath, not because she walked faster than him, but because he was overweight and out of shape. This cuck was dressed like a little boy, in a blue sailor shirt that didn't quite fit him. Hollis Hillman was a special kind of preacher that liked to accuse anyone who disagreed with him on anything, to be a 'Calvinist,' which was the highest insult in his warped, little mind.

"Why did I ever sleep with you?" the former astronaut asked her, huffing and puffing as if they had just fucked.

"I don't know, Hollis. Why did you? Oh, that's right, it was because I let you shove a silver spoon up my nubile, 15-year-old, ass."

"I certainly wasn't tantalized by that sublime heart you don't have," he answered bluntly, after stopping and bending over to grab his trembling knees, which felt like they were about ready to give out. "I should've known you'd prove to be a goddamn Calvinist." While he sounded as if he were trying to cough up a lung, she walked the rest of the way to the wheezing man's car. Suddenly, she picked up on the fact that she was being watched. Spinning around in anger, she caught glimpse of and made visual contact with her admirer.

Brooke had cast a bewitching spell over Wolf as he watched her turn to look him in the eye. He wasn't attracted to her in the least, as he could smell the perfume of evil on her, but still…he couldn't bring himself to look away. Something about her made it impossible to resist staring at her. And as she offered him a wide smile, he saw her pearly whites eerily turn into razor-thin fangs. Her enchanting brown eyes changed to a piercing yellow color, but not like his. Her eyes were distinctively feline. This image of her burned into Wolf's memory, as he watched her scratch the word, *pussy*, into the side of the man's *Mercury Cougar*, using nothing but her fingers. Wolf, as enthralled as he was by her, shut his eyes just for a moment, hoping that when he reopened them, she'd prove to be an optical illusion.

As he relaxed his blinked eyelids, he saw that the malevolent mirage was gone. Just as he took a breath of relief, he was startled by Brooke popping up on the driver's side of the Van. She was staring back at him now, through Cheri's window, still with that spooky Cheshire grin. Her eyes were wide open, and Wolf's hair stood straight up on its ends, as if he had been struck by lightning. Wolf closed his eyes one more time, and this time, when he opened them back up, Brooke was gone. No trick this time. She had disappeared without a trace, and Wolf wasn't complaining. Brooke had given cats a bad name, just like too many Christians have done to Christ.

Out of nowhere, a stunning woman came up and sat across from Cheri at her booth. This naked lady had long, straight blonde hair; not dirty blonde, but a shimmery, fairy blonde. Her head was dressed with a crown of beautiful flowers…flowers which were immune to death or decay. She was very easy on the eyes, with aerodynamic features and the body of a *Sunset Blvd* stripper. However, as beautiful as she was, she didn't hold a candle to Dawn…at least not in Cheri's eyes. The only thing that let Cheri know that she wasn't human was the woman's tail. She had the tail of a cow, which came out of her backside, just above her butthole. She spoke to Cheri in rhymes.

"Don't continue this journey," she warned Cheri. "I know you care for the Cherokee whore, but this pursuit will not fare well for you. It will end badly, and only bring grief and gore."

"I'm sorry, who are you?" the curious Cheri asked the pretty intruder, while she held her fork in front of her, in mid-shovel, and glared at the odd woman who had interrupted her meal.

"My given name is, Huldra. I have no home to speak of. I am despised by God, and have no man to love. I can live my life in eternal beauty and be the desire of every male. Or, I could have sex, gain the strength of ten men, and lose my tail." Then, as abruptly and as strangely as she had inserted herself into the picture, Huldra got up and walked away from Cheri's booth.

"Okay, that was weird," Cheri said to herself, out loud, before going back to dining, as if nothing had happened and no warning had been delivered.

Cheri scooped a handful of the pistachio-based pudding in her hand, and began rubbing it all over her face. She could feel the nuts and mini marshmallows massage her skin, as she washed herself in the acidic pineapple juice. Some patrons stared at her as if she was a certifiable nutcase, while others gazed upon her as if she was simply enjoying her meal by playing with her food. When management saw what she was doing and noticed the scene she was making, he offered her a free steak to take with her, on the condition that she immediately leave the establishment and never return. Cheri brought the doggy bag back to Wolf and let him feast on the juicy rib-eye, while she got them back on the road. Wolf never mentioned the creepy cat-lady that he had briefly encountered, who had nearly scared the shit out of him.

As Cheri climbs into her *Dodge* Van, little does she know that she is being watched. A serial rapist, who had caught glimpse of her at the last gas pump, had been following her ever since. He drove a 1965 white *El Camino* with two black stripes on the hood. Her stalker bore a slight resemblance to actor, Burt Reynolds. He had severe slow-transit constipation, so he didn't need to take many rest stops. He also carried a CB radio in his car and had truckers tip him off on where her Van was, when and if he had lost sight of her. He was foolishly tracking her, having no inkling that she traveled with a protective timber wolf. He figured it would only be a matter of time before the right moment would present itself, and he would have his opportunity to take advantage and have his way.

Before Cheri and Wolf got back on the road to resume their quest, she pulled into a different parking space, which was in front of a somewhat shabby theater.

As she and Wolf entered the cinematic venue, the employees immediately got nervous at the sight of Wolf. The manager quickly approached her, but before he could ask her to leave his entertainment business, she made eye contact with him and hypnotically overpowered his feeble mind.

"My friend and I just want to watch a show," she said. "Let us in, and we will leave after we're done."

"Of course, mam," the dimwitted manager replied. "You and your wolf are welcome. Please accept my compliments. Give her anything she wants!" he ordered his speechless staff.

Within minutes, Cheri and Wolf were in the dark theater, waiting for the show to start. Cheri had chosen the movie, *Grease*. The film had actually been released almost a year before, but this theater was in the habit of showing films that had been out for a long time, at a discounted price. The counter refreshments, however, were another story, which made it all the more satisfying for Cheri, who was given whatever she asked at no charge. She sat in the isle seat to be next to Wolf, who shared her humungous tub of popcorn that was covered in salt and imitation butter. There were only a few other people in that theater and once they saw Cheri and Wolf, they wound up watching them instead of the picture. Cheri and Wolf enjoyed the musical film, and soon found themselves near the end. They watched the scene where Sandy and Danny both decide to change who they are for the one they love, so that their love will be returned. Though this wasn't the greatest message, it made Cheri think and seriously consider doing the same. She could never change her heritage, but she was determined to change in whatever ways she could.

Meanwhile, Dawn is stark naked, still confined in the same damp prison with the other snatched captives. She had been sold by the batshit, Richard Ramirez, to an underground black market. She hadn't had a shower since being bathed and violated by the traffickers, who had roughly scrubbed and molested her, and then rinsed her off with a fire hose. Her body had been deloused, gang raped, beaten by police batons, bruised, and weakened from dehydration and starvation. Because Dawn had been robbed of her strength, she had surrendered all hope of being spared from this dilemma. If she refused to do what they demanded, they would make her suffer, and she knew she was in no shape to fight. If she submitted to everything they told her to do, it would show them that she was weak, which would only make their job easier and more fulfilling. No matter what she did or didn't do, she would be punished and forsaken. Dawn fought to keep her head above water, but it was becoming more and more difficult.

Sitting in her dark cell, she had a ton of time to let her thoughts wander. As she waited for the persecutors to come for her again, she came to a revelation that she had somehow missed until now. Mathias (aka: *Alexei*) was born with a German name, but never claimed to have, nor was ever heard speaking with, a German accent. Reuben, on the other hand, bragged about his *thick German accent*, which he never once showed any evidence of. As Dawn's mind drifted back to her brief romance with Reuben, she wondered how she never picked up on this before. This, of course, only credited her love for Reuben, as a detail like this wouldn't have escaped her otherwise. How did she not notice that Reuben never used any broken English? She couldn't remember there being any German slang or dialect mixed in with his American language. His *W's* sounded like *W's*, not *V's*. He didn't make his *V's* sound like *F's*, or his *Th's* sound like *Z's*. She also realized that his *D's* should have sounded more like *T's*. His *R's* should have been soft to nonexistent. Come to think of it, Reuben didn't have a German accent at all. Was she crazy? Was he? Had he been delusional or deceptive? Was he even German? She couldn't even recall him clearing his throat or sounding like he was coughing up flem? Did he lie to her about who he was or where he was from? Or, was he simply an unhinged lunatic?

"Well, we did meet in a mental hospital," she said aloud to herself, as if to explain anything that was a bit ill-advised or illogical, with where and how they had been introduced.

Dawn also thought about how instantly they had fallen for each other. Their connection had been an immediate one, which she also chalked up to them being in a psychiatric ward. Did she regret her time with Reuben? Not in the least, or in any shape or form. Their courtship had been unorthodox and unconventional, and there were things about Reuben that made little to no sense, but she knew their love had been real. Nothing about their relationship, as peaked and peculiar as it was, had been a ruse, and that was why she was still so hung up on him. He genuinely loved her and she him, and that was all that mattered to her. Nothing would ever change that or take that away from her, not even her own disturbed mind or his premature death. He may have been a crackpot, a nutcase, and a madman in every other way, but his love for her wasn't a pretense or a charade, and that was all she needed to know.

The steel door to the underground prison opens up, and a steroid-pumped goon drags in a rabid wolf that had been hunted, butchered, and imported especially for her. It was easy for the traffickers to have access to exotic animals, as their ring was socially linked to unpardonable groups that shamelessly made their money from poaching, trophy hunting, and other moral turpitude against wildlife. This, sadly, was a common denominator for many corporations and organizations, both religious and secular.

"You, son of a bitch!" Dawn screams, from seeing the mangled corpse of the innocent animal, and filled with seething fury towards her sadistic captors whom she knew were getting off on tormenting her; which they were succeeding in ways they weren't even consciously mindful of.

The brutish thug runs up and kicks the alpha female upside the face with his steel-toe boots, knocking out a few of Dawn's teeth and nearly taking her pretty head off. The Muslim ruffian laughs at her, as the livid but frightened squaw fearfully cringes in the corner of the stone-walled cell. The hired bully closes and bolts the door behind him, leaving Dawn to stare at the decomposing, maggot laced, and fly infested wolf. Dawn briefly slips into a daydream state, where she imagines herself pouncing on the Islamic goon, gouging his eyes out and then eating them. This amusing hallucination was short-lived, as the mere thought of tasting his detestable flesh sickened her to the very core.

She didn't want to feast off the contaminated beast, as it immediately reminded her of her dear friend that she had regretfully deserted. Then again, it had already been slaughtered by other hands, and her insatiable hunger was quickly overpowering her conscience and values. It chilled Dawn to know that after all the horror she had been through in her past, nothing had been more morbid or macabre than this damned situation. These people rejoiced in the exquisite suffering of others, and she found nothing to be more terrifying. She wrapped her arms around herself, as if shivering, and rubbed her injured arms. She wished that Cheri would come looking for her, not knowing that she already was and had been.

"It's just an animal," Claire said, showing her insensitive and inconsiderate nature. "It's not like they have souls."

"That's ridiculous," Dawn said, remembering her father's sermons and listening to her heart. "Animals aren't put on this planet for our sadistic amusement. Animals are sacred, and should be treated with respect. Jesus Christ is often referred to as the *Lamb of God* and the *Lion of Judah*. These symbols meant something. Jesus is called the *final sacrifice* for several reasons, not just one. Animals matter too, and aren't we the real animals by not valuing or respecting them?"

"So, I take it you don't approve of hunting as a sport?" Stacey asked, already safely assuming Dawn's answer.

"It's not a sport, unless the animals are armed too. Hunting is as cowardly an act as abortion. Both are crimes against the helpless," Dawn said, as she worried about Wolf and hated herself for not being there to protect him. "The dove is a symbol of peace and purity, which signifies the personality of the Holy Ghost. Any preacher or minister who advocates hunting is not only no man of God, but is a bloodthirsty sociopath. Jesus was a pacifist, not a sadist. When Daniel was placed into the lion's den, he was unharmed. If he had been placed in a den of conservative Christians, I guarantee you that the outcome would have had a far different result."

"God says, *do not kill*," Julie added.

"That's right, Julie. Matthew 5:21 and 19:18 tell us to not murder. The Bible doesn't say, *do not murder people*. It says, *do not murder*. Very good, Julie," Dawn complimented her, impressed with Julie's heart. "Genesis 9:5 says that every beast (including humankind) has the same lifeblood. It's all precious. Exodus 20:13 says, *do not kill*, period. God also wouldn't have made such an effort to have Noah rescue two of each animal, if the Lord didn't care about them. God postponed the Flood so that the animals could be saved."

Julie cowered in a ball, sitting with her knees up and her arms wrapped around her legs. Her head was down, hiding her face from the other girls. She was proud of Dawn's words, but had an uneasy time around any kind of conflict or confrontation. She was in her teens, but still had the mind and maturity of a preschooler. Her voice was somewhat muffled because of how she sat, but she wanted to voice her support for Dawn's stance against animal cruelty, and Dawn deeply respected her for that.

"Who was that?" Dawn asked the other girls, referring to the hostile bully who had just relieved her of some of her teeth.

"That's, Boner," Claire answered. "We hear he moonlights as an owner of a Christian bookstore and the band leader for his Baptist church."

"He's an uber-prick, disguised as a Christian," Karen added, while inadvertently describing the vast majority of the so-called *Christian community*.

Mathias and Joy had stopped at a convenience store, after filling their tank. Mathias had outgrown his appeal, but she was afraid to take his life. As an Arae, she was bound by certain rules that she couldn't change or control. Initially conjured to wreak havoc on those who tormented the late Aleister Crowley, she needed to remain connected to his worshippers if she wanted to endure on Earth and in human form. Joy picked up a straw broom and was playing with it inappropriately between her legs. The ELO song, *Evil Woman*, plays in the background. Before she knew it, Joy was pretend-riding the broom handle, as if she were competing in a witch's rodeo. A few men stared at her in lust, while others were afraid to make eye contact, but nobody approached her, as she gave off a clear and present vibe of danger. One man, however, had the balls to speak his mind and tell her what he thought of her.

"You're a freak," he rudely muttered, with neither courtesy or compliment behind his words.

"If only you knew," Joy said back. "If you only knew."

MAY 6, 1979
HARE MOON

The Islamic thug, who was jacking off to making Dawn suffer, was unfortunately not the only oppressor behind this real-life nightmare. Boner was just one of many perpetrators that were employed in this barbarous syndicate, and the only one who wasn't fair-skinned. These were human fleas who thrived off the misery of others, while enjoying being the cause of it. These were human predators who were the scum and scourge of the Earth, somewhere between identity thieves and terrorists. There was power and wealth funding this underground operation, which was how they were able to get away with murder. These sordid monsters solicited girls for much worse than simple prostitution. These bloodsucking ticks were prominent members of society and pillars of their communities.

Clients would take these girls to parties, for those who had just gotten elected into office, as arm candy. These clients included cops, evangelists, politicians, shrinks, ministers, judges, and sports team owners. The girls were taught how to hold prestigious conversations and were trained how to be ladies in public. Later, when they were alone with the clients, heinous horrors would happen behind the closed doors. They were sat upon and smothered, as a form of torture. Sometimes they were forced to have sex with boys as young as 5, while the voyeurs pleasured themselves. Each client had different expectations, and if any of the girls dared put up a struggle or disobey in any way, the whole lot of them would be severely disciplined for the misbehavior of one. Punishment would often range from forcing the girls to eat dog feces, to tying them up and electrocuting them.

Jonah T. Clark and Brandon Morgans are watching Howard Cosell host, *Battle of the Network Stars*. They both had impeccable backgrounds, just like the spotless *Boner*, who had no criminal record. Jonah is wearing a Hawaiian shirt with huge collars, and Brandon is donning a *Polo* shirt with sweater sleeves tied around his neck. These two preppy bullies lounged back with their feet propped up, watching the boob tube, while five young women starved in lockup only five yards away. The girls could hear the television, and listened to their jailers laugh and enjoy the celebrity competition, when all they had to watch was each other's tears.

"Wasn't Pat Boone on this last year?" Jonah asked.

"No, I think that was Debby Boone." Brandon responded.

"Who cares? Those religious types are all the same. Uptight, upscale, outrageously overpaid assholes," Jeff said, just coming back from picking up some supplies at Rev. Eli's church.

"Why are you always so damned negative?" Jonah asked. "Stop being so negative! This is why we don't talk to you, because you're so damned negative."

"Yeah, Jeff *Shh-Liar*," Brandon added, purposely poking fun at Jeff's last name, which he felt had an appropriate pronunciation.

"Umm, I think you have the words *negative* and *honest* mixed up," Jeff Schleyer replied, as he reached up to adjust the sweatband on his forehead.

Jeff suddenly froze, standing behind his two co-workers, while joining them in drooling over the luscious Hollywood babes on the televised athletic event. Donna Pescow (from *Saturday Night Fever*), Susan Richardson (from *Eight is Enough*), Toni Tennille (from *The Captain & Tennille* variety show), Brianne Leary (from *CHiPs*), Mary Crosby (from *Dallas*), and Valerie Bertinelli (from *One Day at a Time*) were some of the sitcom queens who were causing them to shove their hands down their pants.

Stacey was the same age as Dawn and had spent her entire life there, as a sex slave. Her parents had actually sold her to the ring, while she was still an infant. So, she had been bred for this, and had known nothing different or better from life. Stacey wasn't all there, mentally. She never actually spoke like a regular person or engaged in normal conversation. She could talk, and knew the

English language, but all she ever did was ask questions…literally.

Karen had just turned 16. She had been abducted from her family while she was just a baby. Someone had lifted her out of a shopping cart, at a *Wal-Mart*, while her mother was flirting with one of the store managers. As she threw herself at him, he saw her baby be stolen from the basket, but never said a word to the promiscuous mother or to the police. Karen, much like William had been, prided herself on her exceptional knowledge of the Gospel. One of her jailers had taken pity on her and given her a Bible, so that book became her escape. She would lose herself in the Word and read it until it was committed to memory. Yet, even still, she didn't really know as much as she thought. She, like the broad majority of Christians, tainted the Bible with her own opinions and interpretations, rather than simply believing and accepting what was written there in front of her.

Claire was 19. She had a nasty and angry demeanor, but not without good reason. She was one of the clients who was bought repeatedly, and exclusively, for a very specific purpose. Rich snobs would rent her from the syndicate and she would be whisked away to some remote property or island. She would be set free, temporarily, while being hunted as game. She would often be returned hours, days, or even weeks later, with broken fingers or ribs, or brain damage from having been kicked in the head. The underground facility had a high-profile surgeon on staff, so there was always a medical doctor on premises to tend to these girls when they came back busted. They'd be patched up and given time to heal, just so they could be broken again.

"I'm going to kill myself," Teri said, who was a habitual and pathological liar. Claire and Karen both rolled their eyes, knowing better than to believe anything Teri had to say.

Julie just sat there quietly with her legs crossed, petting an invisible kitty in her lap, which she had named, *Pee Pee*. Her imaginary feline-friend apparently had yellow fur, hence the name she chose to give it. This was also appropriate, considering that Julie often wet herself while she slept. Julie had been kidnapped at age 12, which was 5 years ago. When she was first brought in, she wouldn't stop crying for days, so they stripped her down, handcuffed her wrists behind her back, bound her ankles with restraints, and whipped her back and ass with a switch, until blood rushed from her young flesh. The traffickers then took turns pissing on her open cuts, wounds, and orifices. She was then thrown into a cage that was hung from the ceiling, where they left her isolated for weeks, in solid darkness, with nothing but her own urine to drink. Girls who weren't born into sex slavery tended to have a harder time adjusting, and Julie was no exception. It took them months to break her, but once they did, she cracked and fell backwards into permanent childhood.

Speaking of childhood, Teri was the way she was because of the Hell she went through as a little girl. She didn't have to be abducted or sold into slavery, because her father worked for the trafficking ring and her mother was one of the young women in captivity. Teri's father used to sit her on his lap while his trousers were down, at dinner parties and formal galas, with his stiff dick inside of her. He did this in the open, from her infancy period until she was 9-years-old. He told her that he had to do this, so that she wouldn't fall off his lap and hurt herself. She didn't know any better then, so she believed him and accepted it as normal, even though it hurt every time he poked her. When her age entered into the double digits, she began to wise up to her father's con. When he noticed that she wasn't buying the *safety* story anymore, his excuse changed from *balance* to *philosophy*. He justified it by telling her that she was born to *serve a higher purpose*, which was to succumb to his every need and desire. When she quit believing that load of bullshit, he began to violently rape her, while either smothering her face with a pillow or having her head in a plastic bag. She was 18 now, and treated like the rest of the girls. Teri's post-traumatic stress had led to her taking after her father, in the sense that she had become what she hated the most…a liar, who felt nothing.

As twisted as the male perpetrators were, it was a two-faced bitch by the name of, Wendy Ledford, who secretly ran the entire operation. She led a double life as the Co-Director for a twelve-step ministry, while her husband, Harry, was the Youth Pastor at the same local, evangelical church. These two frauds were very active with the children's and student ministries, and guilty of far more than fondling or defiling babies. Because the people in this reprehensible syndicate were influential and respected members of their community, nobody thought twice or had any reason to suspect them of being the Devil's champions. The sick reality was that this was how it was all over the planet. Human traffickers were often powerful, successful, rich, or charismatic and counterfeit Christians, which was precisely why they always got away with everything they did. They were always people who were in undeserved positions of authority, who sat in Ivory Towers and suppressed those they considered to be beneath them. Even on the rare occasion when charges were brought and scandals were exposed, nothing ever changed and no penalties were ever paid.

When Richard had abducted Dawn and taken her from Mathias and the *Golden Veil* family, he put a crick in their plan. Mathias and Joy mutually wanted Dawn for their own selfish and secret agendas. Neither of them cared for her, but that didn't keep them from wanting her. They were equally and separately obsessed with the scrumptious Native, and had no intention of taking '*no*' for an answer. They both knew that they would inevitably end up subjecting her to one of their human sacrifice rituals, especially if her attitude failed to change and she continued to reject their persistent sexual advances. But, even if Dawn's fate was to ultimately be the recipient of such a brutal and spiteful demise, it didn't change the fact that they weren't ready to lose her. She was taken far too soon, and they were determined to track her down and use her to live out their darkest and most depraved fantasies. Mathias couldn't deal with his failed love spell, which had obviously backfired. His mind was set on retaliating against her and making her pay for her blatant disrespect and disinterest.

They had been travelling West, since leaving Midland, not counting all the times Cheri turned around. Magus Mathias and Joy Zanetti had been following them the whole time, through an electronic toy that Cheri had in the back of her Van. Joy could sense that the *Speak & Spell* was sitting there, and had the supernatural ability to spy on them through this childlike technology. Mathias certainly hadn't forgotten about his vendetta against Dawn for not reciprocating his carnal desires, and attacking her lesbian lover was second best to killing the tribal taco.

While pulled over at a rest area, off *I-19* Southbound, in Green Valley, AZ, Joy quietly opens the back doors of the Van. Cheri is out like a light, dead asleep. Wolf is laying down with her in the back, and perks up when he sees the evil priestess. While Joy uses her pseudo-kindness to try and lure Wolf out, Mathias creeps around to enter the vehicle from the front. His intent is to take Cheri by surprise and sedate her with chloroform. Joy has something hidden behind her back as well, but it's not a rag saturated with a volatile solvent.

Joy had a special skill, where she would use her soft fingers to fondle the head and hair of her chosen victim, effectively lulling them to sleep. Then, with a razor-tipped iron sheath on her middle finger, she would pierce their side and painlessly remove their lung and liver to either eat or use later in rituals. The wound would always heal immediately, without leaving any mark or scar. She planned on doing the same to the already-sleeping Cheri, and could already taste her internal organs on her vile tongue.

Joy and Mathias spray painted a black pentagram on the outside of the Van, which was their way of marking Cheri as their victim and asking that her soul be lost after they snuffed her life. Little did they know that Cheri, like Joy, was part demon and had no chance of redemption or hope of salvation. The moon was beaming down on Cheri's van, as if God himself was watching over it. Joy chuckled softly, amused by the beacon of light, as it reminded her of a little-known fact she had learned through the Craft.

"The circle around the five-star pentacle actually represents the moon," Joy whispered to Mathias, as she cautiously climbed into the back of the Van. "It was originally called, *The First Pentacle of Mercury*," she added, struggling not to laugh out loud.

"I know that," the know-it-all Mathias said softly and begrudgingly, annoyed and insulted that Joy had the audacity to try teaching him something or assume that he was ignorant on the matter. "Aleister Crowley was the first to use the inverted pentagram, and was also the one to coin the term, *sex magick*," he added pretentiously, while smiling insincerely at his *Golden* sister and staring at the coveted area between her legs.

As they moved in closer to ambush the resting Cheri, Joy's mouth began to bleed. A single drop of poisonous blood fell off her lower lip and as it impacted the floor of the Van, it sizzled and burned a hole through it, as if it were hydrochloric acid. Wolf saw this toxic drool and watched what it did to the Van. He growled and snarled at Joy, giving her the look of death, as Cheri started to slowly open her eyes. The semi-succubus quickly grabbed Joy by the throat, with her left hand, and attempted to squeeze the very life out of her. Mathias promptly came to Joy's aid, by trying to whack Cheri with a broom handle that had horses' tails tied at the end.

"Revelation 9, bitch. This is your last chance to blow my trumpet," the vulgar Mathias quoted Scripture, but sacrilegiously using it to coerce Cheri into giving him head. "Your delicious friend, Dawn, made the mistake of not jumping on this. Don't let this pass from your lips as well. Come on, pink-haired floozy, give me a try."

Cheri seized hold of Mathias too, also by the throat, using her other hand. Looking straight into his evil eyes, she showed Mathias the harm that he had done to others and to himself. She filled him with a petrifying fear that he had never before felt, as he realized where he was going and the reality of what that meant. For the first time, the religious guru regretted his wasted life of blasphemy.

Cheri looked at Mathias's distasteful tattoo on his forehead. "666, huh? 6 times 3 is 18. Is that why you went after my young girlfriend, asshole? You should really grow some eyebrows…but grow a brain first."

Dawn was obviously not 18 anymore, but the raspberry queen liked to pretend she was. Cheri's eyes became fire, as Mathias burst into flame and was reduced to ash. Cheri quickly brought her free hand to Joy's throat, as the Arae wasn't going to go quite as easily.

Cheri couldn't understand why Joy was so strong and so resilient to her demonic powers, until she looked into her eyes and saw that she wasn't alone in her infernal roots. She opened wide her mouth and blew fire, much like a dragon would, in Joy's face. Yet, the flames had no effect, and didn't do so much as singe a single hair on Joy's impervious head.

"That's right, bitch," Joy said, "you've messed with the wrong…"

"What do you want?!" Cheri interrupted her.

"Your precious arm candy," Joy said back, smiling.

Cheri was horrified, not having seen this coming. "Dawn? You're after Dawn?"

"Where is she?" Joy demanded. "Tell me, and I will spare your pathetic life."

"Dawn's taken," Cheri said boldly and confidently, realizing that she might have met her match, but willing to die before helping this monster snatch her lover away.

"Hahahaha!" Joy cackled in a scary voice, as they continued trying to strangle each other. "Do you honestly believe that Dawn could love you? You're a fucking demon!"

"So are you," Cheri responded calmly but firmly.

"Yes, but I'm not in love with her. I want to ravish her, and then ravage her when I'm done. I will poison her with the deadly, purple plant known as, *Wolf's Bane*, and laugh as I watch her wither away in indescribable agony. I will consume her very soul after I have my way with her tasty flesh."

"I don't think so," Cheri refuted. "Not if I have anything to say about it."

"Oh yeah?" Joy asked. "What are you going to do to stop me? Huh? What are you going to do?"

Cheri stuck her hand down the front of Joy's pants and grabbed her firmly by the crotch, sticking her middle finger up the Crowleyan's dried cunt.

"Fight fire with fire!" Cheri yelled, as she set her own hand on fire, which in turn caused Joy's vagina to combust. "By the power of three times three, let her reap what she has sown! So mote it be! This evil bitch is overthrown!" Cheri yells, using Joy's own witchcraft against her.

The fire rapidly spread throughout Joy's body and eventually overpowered her will. Joy screamed in unspeakable agony, as she burned alive right there, while Cheri continued to choke her neck and squeeze her diseased throat.

"Go to Hell!" Joy screamed, just before she exploded into a blazing ball of flames.

"You first," Cheri said, as her eyes and hand both returned to normal. "You first." She turned and looked at Wolf, who had jumped out of the Van and been watching from a safe distance. "Now that's what I call a burning bush," Cheri said, cackling in victory and satisfaction.

Like Cheri, the Van had also somehow gone completely unharmed, as if it were supernaturally flame retardant. Wolf timidly but eagerly walked up to Cheri, upon witnessing the flammable fatality that had occurred between the two boogey-women. Wolf had been able to see Joy's nefarious nature when he initially laid eyes on her, and was relieved to see her defeated. The pitch blackness had emanated off of Joy like a darkened cloak of charcoal mist. Yet, there was something endearing about Cheri that he couldn't fully identify, in spite her Cambion legacy. Though Cheri had something in common with Joy, Wolf could see that she was different. Without Cheri touching it or turning the key, the radio magically came on in her Van. The song, *Spooky*, by Atlanta Rhythm Section, played through her Van's speakers.

The inconsolable Dawn had just suffered another nightmare, which felt a bit too real. While brooding over her lingering resentment towards Cheri, she had drifted towards the borders of sleep. She imagined herself casting off all restraints and going berserk, indiscriminately slaying everything and everyone in her path. The ancient, Nordic myth rose before her, and introduced itself as, *Fenrir*. She immediately felt a curious drawing-out sensation from her solar plexus, and there beside her was an oversized wolf. It was a well-materialized, ecto-plasmic form. It was gray and colorless, and had weight, but was clearly not a physical being. She could distinctively feel its back pressing up against her as it lay beside her on the floor, as a large dog might.

"The condition between sleeping and waking is where the etheric double readily extrudes," a voice said, which was unseen, but appeared to be coming from the wolf-like apparition.

Dawn wakes once again in her dungeon, which is appropriately shaped like a wigwam. It was dim and damp, and was equipped with a toilet but no sink. Her bone choker had been ripped away and destroyed in front of her. Since she was taken out of isolation and placed with these other girls, who had all been broken through blunt violence, deprivation, intimidation, and savage sexual assault, they had become family. These girls were all consumed with terror and were all of tender age. The other girls had attached themselves to Dawn, turning to her for comfort and looking up to her as the alpha. Dawn's heart wrenched for her cellmates, as she could literally feel their pain and actually feel their thoughts and fears. Dawn tried to be maternal for them, but the truth was she was secretly just as scared. Julie approached Dawn and offered her a necklace, which was similar to the one Bruce Lee had worn. It had a wolf tooth hanging from the black cord.

"Please," she said, "take my necklace, to replace the one that they took from you." Though Julie's heart was in the right place, her necklace…much like her yellow kitten…was imaginary.

Dawn wept softly, as Julie's sweet gesture moved her, emotionally. She stretched her arms toward the young girl and brought her in for a warm hug. As she held the empathetic girl up against her naked bosom, she thought about where they were and what the intentions were of the abductors. This was an underground human market, and these girls were being trained to be sold as sex slaves…or worse. Every bone in Dawn's body wanted to rain down genocide on the traffickers, but because of Joy's curse, her strength was gone. She felt the way she did after being intimate with Cheri, but ten times weaker and what appeared to be permanent.

"The night is always darkest before the dawn," the young blonde said, trying to be optimistic and lift Dawn's spirits by attempting to make her laugh. Dawn smiled kindly at Julie and kissed her gently on the forehead, showing her grateful appreciation.

Later that night, the girls had gathered around Dawn and once again fallen asleep with her, as if she was their mother and they her cubs. Julie snuggled up in the alpha's welcoming arms, not even minding the armpit stench that came from Dawn not being able to wash up. Dawn had another lucid dream, after meditating again on those she had lost to tragedy. She was standing, buck naked, in a glamorous garden that stretched the walls of imagination. Reuben stood in front of her, whom Dawn was initially over the moon with bliss to see again, but this euphoria wouldn't last. He peeled her skin from her navel to her head, as if lifting up a shirt. As he did this, he unveiled an elderly woman underneath. Dawn, for the first time, was terrified of her lupine alter ego. Reuben then told her something that disturbed her even more.

"Sweetheart, had our son lived, he would have inherited your curse and lived as a werewolf for the first seven years," he told her. "This would have taken a toll on Donnie, which would have been far greater than your suffering, since his lycanthropy would have afflicted him at such a young age. Because he died at birth, his soul is in a better place. All children are welcomed into Paradise." (Matthew 19:14)

Reuben, of course, was talking about her original curse, not the hex that Joy and Mathias had slayed her with. Dawn was pulled back into her body from having projected to the astral plane, and as her spirit reentered her being, she convulsed briefly and subtly before collecting herself and processing what had happened. It traumatized her even further to not be able to extend her out-of-body-experience, but she also knew that she was needed in her dystopian reality. The other girls were either laying on or around her, which left Dawn feeling flattered but fretful. She desperately wanted to deliver these other captives, but she couldn't even save herself. They had quickly come to see her as a maternal substitute, but Dawn didn't know how to deal with that. Joy's curse had made her feeble and frail. Dawn had come to fear her own shadow, and had regretfully abandoned her support system and lost her only means of defense.

JUNE 11, 1979
MEAD MOON

Witches believe that their bodies aren't sinful, but sacred. This is precisely why it's so easy for sociopathic and psychopathic women to screw over those they pretended to love without an ounce of remorse or regret. This is why it's too easy for narcissistic women to leave relationships and marriages without shedding a tear or suffering a second thought. Though Cheri was part demon, and though she had originally used Dawn for selfish reasons, she wasn't void of humanity. She knew that profiting from the misery of others was wrong, which is why she wasn't interested in marriage (which wasn't an option for her anyway, since it was still illegal for gays and lesbians to have this right). Witches feel that they are born perfect, and therefore have no real need for inferior men, other than for carnal entertainment, financial gain, and mass reproduction. Cheri was half demon, but she was no witch, and not nearly as wicked as so many women out there who play men for profit, babies, or just the demented pleasure of hurting them. Cheri wasn't proud of her origin, and was deeply ashamed of her roots, which only further inspired and motivated her to ensure that her ending was different.

Cheri had spent her childhood in various foster homes, never connecting with any family she was paired with. This was merely one element of her history that made her feel alone and isolated. No matter how many times the nuns blessed over her, or how much effort social workers invested into making her seem normal and well-adjusted, they just couldn't change her. Cheri was Cheri, and even though being herself only got her shunned, she knew who she was and that was enough. Dawn had made her want to be a better person, and gave her reason to love someone more than herself. For this, if nothing else, she owed the Cherokee beauty a debt of gratitude that she fully intended to pay. Her eyes were droopy and heavy, as she struggled and squinted to see the road before her. She was languid and lethargic, and her eyes were sore and red. Cheri looked back at Wolf, who was curled up behind her, on the floor.

"If it wasn't for you, I don't know if I could do this," she told him, knowing he was fast asleep.

Cheri adored Dawn, but their unwanted separation had left her drained, both health-wise and otherwise. She tried to stay strong, so she could save her trophy-princess, but couldn't help but be thankful for Wolf. Just by being there with her, he kept her from giving into the temptation to just lie down and collect bed sores.

"The Bible says, *this too shall pass*," an invisible voice said from on top of her right shoulder.

"The Bible says no such thing," Cheri said aloud to the voice who wasn't there. "If it did, it would be a blatant falsehood. Anyone who has lived long enough knows that pain never ends, but is only replaced or compounded with other pain."

The family in the back huddled closer together, fearful for their lives and nervous after watching Cheri talk to herself. She had abducted them in a hotel parking lot, as they were coming out to their car. Cheri needed funding for their rescue mission, and since she didn't have any money left, she decided to do whatever it took to make it work. She picked the family that were dressed the snazziest and looked the part. Once she had acquired the father's wallet, she knew she had chosen wisely. The man begged her to let his wife and two children go, but she knew she couldn't do that. She knew that they would cancel their credit cards and go straight to the police. No, as much as Cheri wanted to do right by them, she couldn't do so without risking too much and sacrificing her reunion with Dawn. She needed the money, and the family would have to pay in more ways than one. They weren't walking away from this and they all knew it. They didn't know who to be scared of more, the pink-haired basket case or the white wolf sleeping in the back with them.

Signs, the song by Five Man Electrical Band, played through as Cheri read the many signs on the freeway, some of which were there and others that were simply imagined. Obnoxiously long traffic lights provoked Cheri's shameless and unfiltered use of profanity, while she became more unhinged without her beloved Dawn to keep her grounded. Thoughts swim through Cheri's head, as she imagines the worst and swears to erase whomever she needs to in order to retrieve Dawn.

Hours later, Cheri's van unexpectedly breaks down on the side of the road. The *check engine* light is on, which understandably never seizes to stir up feelings of wrath and rage. Feeling vexed, she and Wolf get out and start walking to the next *Exit*. They eventually reach a small automotive garage, where they quickly get hassled and harassed.

"Somebody call *Animal Control*!" one of the brain-dead mechanics shouts out.

"We need one of you to come take a look at our Van," Cheri said, ignoring the grease monkey's intentional insult.

"Sure thing, mama," one of the other not-so-wise men blurted out. "What are you going to give me in return?"

Cheri looked at him and grinned, before gently shutting her eyes and meditating on his face. She then used her pyro-kinetic powers to start a fire inside his skull. As she calmly kept her eyes closed, she could hear the man scream in agony for several minutes until his head finally combusted into flames. Cheri opened her eyes just in time to see him drop to the floor. His two co-workers held their heads in petrifying fear that she would do the same to them.

"Now," Cheri started again, "who wants to help us get back on the road?"

Not only do they comply with her wishes, but they do so in haste, making her Van their urgency and priority. The third mechanic, who had been silent this whole time, convinces Cheri to come to a *key party* at his house. She agrees to go and follows him home, once he clocks out. Her stalker's '65 *El Camino* is there. When they walked into the house, there was a cluster of a dozen swingers sitting avidly in the living room. The percentage of each gender was equal to the other.

"Just put your Van keys in the big glass bowl," he instructed her. The other party-goers were engaged in a heavy group discussion about the Manson murders.

"The Manson Family murders were inspired by a plagiaristic crime committed by Dennis Wilson. The *Beach Boys* stole one of Charlie's songs and took credit for it."

"To make matters worse, Terry Melcher had promised to make things right by signing Charlie, only to break his word, claiming that Charlie had real potential but that his original material was unmarketable," another contributed to the dialogue.

"I know, right? This was clearly bullshit, considering who Terry Melcher was and what he had done for others," the former beatnik ranted, sporting a bleached jean jacket, which had an all-black, artistic portrait of Manson's spooky mug on the back.

"You do know that Charlie is a bigot, don't you? That whole *Helter Skelter* thing was a race war that Charlie convinced his disciples was coming," said one of the other men in the group.

"Actually, that's a corruption of the truth. Charlie only began talking about that whole idea after Tex Watson had the girls help him kill Sharon Tate. The *race war* was merely Charlie's way of trying to keep the pigs from sniffing them out. They were already hounding him for grand theft auto, but that didn't worry him the way that the murders did. The whole *Helter Skelter* concept was just a front…a distraction…to hide what Charlie didn't want to be known."

Soon, the small talk was over, and the polite chit chat had been replaced by lustful stares and crossed fingers. Everyone in attendance was there to knock boots and sweat bullets, not engage in heavy, social conversation. Each person got up, one at a time, and walked over to the bowl, hoping for their first choice. As the bedroom eyes grew hungrier and wilder, Cheri soon found it to be her turn. Cheri ironically takes the keys that belong to the *El Camino*, and ends up accompanying the driver upstairs, having no idea that he had been stalking her since laying eyes on her at that one gas station. Not only would she soon learn what a creep he was, but this chance hookup would rid the world of a cunning snake.

Cheri thought back to when she was 10. The year was 1945, and she had just been returned to the boarding shelter. Her hair was kept short, and her bangs were neatly trimmed and cut straight across. The clothes she wore were secondhand, cheap, and plain. The War was coming to a close and welfare professionals were doing all they could to shut down orphanages. Caseworkers loved seeing children suffer, particularly when they could contribute to their pain. The Christian community pretended to care on the surface, but never did anything truly helpful unless it benefited the church. Rumors were making their rounds, and word had it that every orphanage would either be converted to a retirement home for the elderly or be turned into a psychiatric facility for kids who are mentally disturbed. She recalled this one girl who wouldn't stop pressing her buttons, that finally got a reaction out of her when she shoved Cheri and pulled her hair, only to wind up with third-degree burns on her arms and neck.

Meanwhile, Agent Shelling was getting his fill of grief from the press, as the media was becoming more impatient and intolerant with the Bureau's distinct lack of results. He didn't have the energy or the heart to tell them that he was shut down and washed up, and that the FBI couldn't give a shit anymore about finding Dawn.

So, to avoid any awkwardness or explanation, he played along as if he were still actively pursuing public enemy number one.

"Has she called in, to taunt you or make any demands? Do you suspect any involvement with a religious sect? Is she a devoted disciple of an unholy army of Satanic warriors? Is she part of the *Illuminati* or *The New World Order*?" the relentless reporter asked preposterous questions, aiming for a fantastical twist of sensationalism for his absurd article.

"If she ever calls, we will trace it," the disgruntled Agent lied. "And that bold act will be the harbinger of our salvation. If she's in a Christian cult or a Satanic coven, we will dismantle her network," he answered, sighing. "Trust me, you will know something when the FBI does."

"Has there been any major arrests in the case? Any leads at all? Any co-conspirators?" he pressed the unemployed Fed, unwilling to take a hint and determined to get something from him that he could spice up. He was all about exploiting and exaggerating, and the Agent knew it.

"No," Agent Shelling slowly shook his head. "We know who she is. The name of the perp isn't in question. It's just her whereabouts that are still unknown."

"You've taken no one into custody?!" the reporter antagonized, as if to imply that it would be better that they arrest anyone, even if that person isn't suspicious or guilty. Agent Shelling swallowed in relation, as he couldn't deny that he had once resonated with this sick mentality.

"Dawn Moon is exiled, and will eventually have no other option but to seek refuge. I would imagine that she may already need medical attention," Shelling responded, hinting that they will grab her the minute she checks in to a hospital. "The authorities, nationwide, are cooperating with the Federal Bureau. The more she rains Hell upon the world, the more evidence she'll leave behind that will lead to her inevitable capture," he lied again. Agent Shelling's obsession with Dawn had long faded. She was too elusive and too clever, and he had grown weary of restlessly searching for her without any results. He started to wonder if there was more to her disturbing past that made her what she became. He loved his wrecked sister and deceased nephew, but he had just grown tired of dismal failure. He felt like he had been chasing a ghost, and just couldn't do it any longer. His anger and hatred had mutated into doubt and defeat.

As the hair-raising stalker groped Cheri on the bed, and played with and fondled all three of her nipples, he grew more aggressive every minute that she allowed the heavy petting to go on.

"Stop," she demanded, with a stern face. "Just stop."

"What?" he asked back. "What's the problem?"

"You. I can't do this. You're making me sick."

"It's a bit late for that. Once you walked into this room, you gave up control. You surrendered the right to be picky," he informed her, still grabbing her by the back of the hair and forcefully sucking on the side of her neck, doing his best to leave the blackest hickey he could. As he marked his territory on her preferred flesh, she gave him one final opportunity to be reasonable and obedient.

"Stop. I'm telling you one last time," Cheri warned.

Posing as if he would finally comply to her wishes, he let go of her momentarily and misled her by acting as if he had calmed down and had second thoughts. This was, of course, a total ruse, as he was completely comfortable with raping her. He had trailed her long enough to know that she had broken the law and therefore knew she had no desire to consort with the police. He looked up at her, with a wicked grin, and put her in her place by putting his foot down.

"Listen, bitch, think of this as a gambling debt. I didn't sign you up for this or hold a gun to your head. You came here voluntarily, thereby silently consenting to an unspoken contract. You're going to get fucked tonight and you're going to like it. Or, perhaps, if you're really not interested in me, we can make other arrangements?"

"Meaning what, exactly?" she inquired, knowing damn well that he had no intention of letting her off the hook, but still curious to see what his asinine answer would be.

"That's a nice wolf you got out there," he said, in the creepiest voice possible, as his breathing got even heavier. "What do you say you turn him over to me and I fuck his brains out, before I gut him from his throat to his dick and fry me up some Wolf burgers?"

It was at that moment that the rest of the house heard a horrifying scream, at a pitch that made the little hairs on their skin stand at attention. This scream wasn't because he had discovered her third nipple, but because he had fucked with the wrong bitch. Cheri strutted out of that bedroom, leaving a pile of burnt ash on the bedspread. The ash was on her arms, hands, and face. She smelled of death…his death. She walked down the winding staircase, while holding the rail as she descended. The homeowner stood at the bottom and pointed a loaded pistol at her head.

"Stop!" he commanded, "or I'll shoot! I swear, I will! I'll do it!" he threatened.

"Go ahead," she calmly gave permission, calling his bluff, while completely relaxed and unconcerned.

The frightened man pulled the trigger, only to hear a harmless noise that was much different than what he had expected it to sound like. The gun hadn't kicked back or sounded violent in the least. He looked down at his hand and to his amazement, saw that his Beretta *Tomcat* had turned into a *Mattel* cap gun. Cheri lifted the man's body off the floor and threw him back into his living room, using nothing but telekinesis. She considered leaving the house in a fiery blaze, but decided that the only one there who deserved to die had already been exterminated. So, she left the domestic hedonism event with only a departing smile and a middle finger.

"Well, that's a humdinger," one of the naked partygoers said, as he and his evening mistress peered through one of the bedroom windows. He wasn't the host, but he had also been born with a silver spoon in his mouth. They watched Cheri climb into her Van, where Wolf was waiting and watching for her, and pull out into the hungry road.

Dawn kept smacking herself in the head and pulling out her hair, trying to force out the unwanted wicked thoughts that she didn't want to admit to thinking. She could feel herself slipping further into madness, and lose what little bit of humanity she had left. She had the insatiable craving to kill, and it no longer mattered who her victims were or if they were among the few she cared about. Dawn grinded and gnashed her teeth, shaking her head and fiercely blinking her eyes. She loved the idea of mass murder, and hated herself because of it. The girls could see Dawn losing her mind in front of them. Julie begged her to stop hurting herself, until Dawn finally brought her hands down and opened her eyes…only to further scare the living shit out of her cellmates. They respected Dawn, but could see the darkness in her eyes, which was plain as day.

"Who agrees with me that Dawn needs a therapist?" Stacey asked out loud, not thinking before she spoke.

"Yeah, or…maybe…a pastor?" the kidnapped Karen suggested, throwing her high-and-mighty two cents in.

"A therapist would only make her worse, not better," Claire enlightened. "What do you get when you put a space between the *e* and the *r*, in *therapist*?"

"*The rapist*," Julie answered, swallowing her own saliva and nearly choking on it, as her sad eyes swelled up with tears for Dawn.

"That's right," Claire acknowledged, "and preachers are no different than therapists."

Dawn just stood there, once again blinking and squinting in a rapid and violent fashion, as if trying to extinguish her eyes from the Hell that she was seeing. Julie started to approach her, wishing to give her a hug, but when Dawn resumed gnashing and grinding her teeth, it made even Julie step back and stay clear from the crazy Indian. Dawn had no intention of hurting Julie or any of the other girls, but as she clenched her fists, she could feel herself losing control, and knew that she would soon have a difficult time restraining herself. Julie looked down at Dawn's fists and saw blood dripping from them. Dawn was digging her nails into her flesh. It was as if Dawn was having a mild stroke or seizure, while Julie and the others felt helpless, not knowing what…if anything…they could possibly do to help her.

JULY 21, 1979
TIN MOON

It was the day after the tenth anniversary of the historic, *Apollo 11*, moon landing. A little boy and his sister were plopped in front of the television, in a middle-class, suburban neighborhood. They had awoken early, excited for the Saturday morning lineup, but their favorite (*Jonny Quest*) didn't come on *NBC* until Noon. They had *Quisp* cereal for breakfast and found a hidden prize in the bottom of the box. The directions on the toy's bag told them to pull the dolphin apart, put baking powder on the inside, and then snap the two pieces back together. This was supposed to make their dolphin dive repeatedly in the water. They had followed these instructions to the letter, after leaving a white trail from the kitchen to the living room carpet. They didn't know what to put the dolphin in, so they put it in the fish tank over by the fireplace. This, of course, only made their white mess a bigger one.

As the unsupervised siblings watched their artificial dolphin bob up and down, an animated commercial played on the TV screen. The citizens of *Toothopolis* were being bombarded by the *Cavity Creeps*. They chanted 'we make holes in teeth,' just before the *Crest*

Team dropped in to save the day. Their sugar-sweetened corn cereal was quickly losing its crunchiness, as the kids had left half their bowls to soak and get soggy in the milk. This was their typical attention span that was also shown by the *Parker Bros.* board game, *Bonkers*, which was often left spread out and forgotten on the floor.

The two grade-schoolers were distracted once again by a noise that was coming from outside. They took their hands out of the now cloudy fish tank and hurried to the big window. Two dogs, who were clearly in heat, were enjoying each other's company in a way that children shouldn't know anything about.

"Fucking bitches," their mother said, after quietly sneaking up behind her excessively curious kids.

The young ones jumped, not having heard their mother come downstairs. She usually slept in till mid-afternoon, not having to work to pay the bills. Their pregnant mother recently had her 5th divorce and lived happily and comfortably from a combination of child support, alimony, state-funded welfare that she somehow astoundingly qualified for, and the money she had fraudulently embezzled from both the government and her exes. This had been her plan all along, unbeknownst to all the foolish men who had fallen for her act and believed in her phony persona. Rebecca often stayed in her cozy robe and fuzzy slippers for most of the day, unless she had to take the children somewhere that required her to begrudgingly get dressed. The children and their mother looked at one another for several minutes, without speaking a word. When the kids turned back to look again at the mating dogs, the three of them were shocked to see what appeared to be a well-dressed homeless man standing outside their window while pressing a *FBI* badge against the glass.

"Let me in," the disheveled man-in-a-suit insisted.

Being the wonderful parent she was, she promptly took her knees off the edge of the sofa, where her kids were standing on, and went to open the front door for the alarming stranger.

Not too long after, Agent Shelling is lounging lazily on the relaxing couch, helping himself to a pastrami and sauerkraut sandwich he'd made in their kitchen. Rebecca and her two children were gagged and bound, sitting in front of him, on the floor. The kids were crying and wrapped back-to-back with duct tape around their little bodies. Rebecca was wide-eyed and terrified, also restrained with duct tape, but only on her wrists and ankles. Shelling had just come back downstairs, after helping himself to the shower. He was now wearing her fancy robe and cozy slippers, which were too small on his big feet. Rebecca was nude and shaking.

"I don't know why I just bathed?" Shelling told her. "I'm going to get dirty again in a few minutes," he said, smiling. "We both are."

"Mmmm!!" she mumbled through the constricting gag, desperately trying to wiggle out of the tape, which was strapped tightly and securely. Her hands were behind her naked back and her efforts to struggle got her nowhere. She knew what was coming, and even though she was shameless in her detached promiscuity, she could tell that this time would be different. He was in control, not her, and she was smart enough to know that it wouldn't be in his best interest to keep them alive after he was done with them.

Meanwhile, Boner was having his usual fun, at the prisoners' expense. He had bought them the Milton Bradley Co. game, *Twister*, where the girls had to use their smooth bodies as playing pieces. They obediently complied, while they sweated on and climbed over each other, trying their best not to fall down. He forced them to play the balance game for hours, no matter how tired they got, as he sat back in a wicker rocking chair and played with himself through his zipper.

"I'm frightened, Dawn," Julie whimpered, as she fought back the tears and noticed that Boner's eyes were particularly zoning in on her body parts.

"Just keep doing what they tell you and don't cause any trouble," Dawn advised her, hoping that her young friend would be okay as long as she listened.

"The fear of the Lord is the beginning of wisdom," Karen said. "The Lord is with me, whom shall I fear? Proverbs 9:10 and Psalm 27:1," she added, as she talked into Julie's open butt crack, who was currently bent over in front of her.

"Somehow, I don't think the Lord is with us," Claire observed. "And, if the Lord doesn't want us to be afraid of our oppressors, then you would think that the Lord would do something to help us."

"Shut your traps, bitches!" Boner yelled in a threatening tone, while continuing to stare and drool over Julie, whom he considered to be the perfect specimen. "No talking, goddammit! Just play the fucking game!"

Boner was sporting brand new, *Studio 54* jeans, while drinking a glass bottle of orange soda. He sat there, singing the *Good Vibrations* song from the *Sunkist* commercial, while a heavy camcorder rested on his shoulder. He taped the girls' activity on a *Betamovie* BMC-100P. This was technology that wouldn't be released for another four years, but was granted to these human traffickers in advance, in exchange for services rendered. Corporate lust was just as enticing and compelling as corporate greed, and the executives at *Sony* were sadly no exception.

Meanwhile, later that same night, Rev. Mingan Moon is being treated at Maryland's *Holy Cross Hospital*, in Silver Spring. He had suffered a stroke that nobody saw coming. After being rushed to the emergency room by his girlfriend and a couple of his male parishioners, no one had come to visit him after they left. As beloved and respected as he saw himself to be, it was a rude awakening to discover that his lovers and followers weren't quite as fond of him as they had long conveyed. Rev. Moon had been there for several days, alone and forgotten. The doctors claimed that they had done all that they could do. They had notified the next of kin after giving up on ever reaching Dawn, and once again, nobody showed.

Mingan laid there on his back, in the uncomfortable hospital bed, watching *Buck Rogers in the 25th Century*, on NBC, on the small TV that came out of the wall. As he watched the on-screen chemistry between Gil Gerard and Erin Gray, the primetime broadcast was interrupted by a loud disturbance of white noise. The stroke he had suffered was major, and the severity still reflected on his face. He looked like a Halloween mask, and though he couldn't budge or speak, he was fully conscious and aware of his surroundings. He watched as the white noise revealed three forbidding characters that were in the shape of voluptuous shadows. As they walked closer and became clearer, the silhouettes crawled out of the boob tube. Within seconds, after a series of flashes and gestures, they stood at the Reverend's bedside.

"We are *Moerae*, the Furies of Fate and the daughters of Nyx," they said in harmony, in a sinister voice that made Mingan lose control of his bowels and mess himself. These beings were unquestionably female, though they bore neither faces or features. Their synchronized voices were also clearly virulent.

Reverend Moon would have cringed and trembled, had he been capable of being mobile. Mingan knew who these curvaceous demons were. He had been visited by the children of eternal night and they had come to collect his soul, which was just as dark as their presence. Though his physical shell was frozen stiff, his black heart began to pound and race, which showed on the electrical monitor. When the nurse's station saw that his chest wires were reading dangerous rates, they immediately rushed to his room, only to find that he had flatlined and been mysteriously altered. A blackness had infected his entire body, as if he had somehow been dyed from the inside out. Dawn's wicked father was gone, and off to star in his own nightmare. The difference between his and Dawn's was that he deserved what was coming.

JULY 31, 1979
HAY MOON

Bored out of their minds, the girls attempt to exchange in witty banter, which is painfully ingenuous and aloof.

"When I break outta here, I'm going to send Boner and his goons up the river!" Teri exclaimed, upset about the unwarranted, unwanted, and excessively thorough cavity search that Boner had just given her.

"How are you going to accomplish that?" Stacey asked.

"Girl, I don't know what land you think you're living in, but this is America. People don't go to prison for being human traffickers. Petty thieves go to prison, who steal to feed their minimum-wage families, who can only get part-time jobs, if that. The criminal element isn't behind bars, it's behind our judicial system," Claire replied cynically but truthfully. "This corporate country is a fucking joke. Evil is never punished here, but rather rewarded. *Land of the free*, my ass."

"This would have never been the America it is today, had the white man not ripped it from our hands. Talk about grand larceny," Dawn said, under her breath.

"Your precious pilgrims were nothing more than common hoodlums."

"The only people who will find themselves in a river is us...and mark my word, it will be a river of tears...our tears...that will wash our hopes and dreams away bit by bit," Julie said, while cradling her imaginary, yellow kitty in her arms.

Dawn once again awoke from her dream, not knowing if what she just saw in her head was a bona fide memory or a fictitious delusion.

Ted Bundy was finally sentenced to death, in the Florida court, after a long, overdrawn period of gross incompetence by the laughable American court system. Tragically, Ted would merely be one of many serial killers who could have been stopped much sooner, had the United States been equipped with ethical authorities and a functional judicial branch.

The girls were grateful to have each other, as they were pretty much left to themselves most of the time. When one of the traffickers would get horny, he'd help himself to one or more of them, or a few of the hired hands would join in on a gangbang. Other than that, they were mainly paid attention to when a client came knocking, or when they needed to be fed (which only happened maybe twice a week, and it was always toxic slop). Then, of course, there was the occasional beating or humiliation, just to keep their jobs exciting.

None of Dawn's cellmates had any idea that she was a feral warrior, who was just stunted and incapacitated because of such noxious jinxing. The girls could see that something was oddly unique about Dawn, but they weren't able to put their finger on it. Dawn was strange but special, scary but sweet, and the girls could all see that. They were all afraid of her, but they also all adored and respected her.

Julie had been gone for a full week, and the other girls worried that she wasn't coming back. Dawn had been especially concerned, having a gut feeling that something terrible had happened to her and that they'd seen the last of their childish and vivacious friend.

"I've had several members of my family commit suicide," Teri falsely claimed, while just secretly wishing out loud.

"Is that really true?" Stacey asked, doing what she does best.

"Oh, please," Claire intervened. "Seriously? Do you think we're that stupid? If anyone should take their own life, it's me. I was bullied mercilessly as a kid, only to be treated like wild game as an adult. My life is a fucking nightmare."

"The Bible says, thou shalt not bear false witness," Karen was more than happy to remind everyone.

"What are you all talking about? Julie is in trouble!" Dawn said, doing her best to put things in proper perspective and keep her cool. "She may be dead, for all

118

we know! God knows what kind of unspeakable horrors are happening to her, as we speak? Yet, all you can do is collectively bitch? Really?! Julie is the sweetest among us. She's so innocent. She's just a little girl, and all you can fucking think about is yourselves!?"

"You're right, Dawn," Karen admitted. "I'm sorry."

"Yeah, me too," Claire also apologized. What she really wanted to say to Dawn was something along the lines of, *well, if you loved Julie so much, why didn't you scissor her while you still had the chance?* but she kept a tight lip. Claire was scathing and sardonic, but she wasn't stupid. She could see something dark in Dawn's eyes that chilled her to the bone.

"I'm sure Julie is okay," Teri lied.

"Are you mad at us?" Stacey asked.

"No," Dawn answered, after taking a deep breath and slowly releasing it. "I'm not mad. I love you guys. I'm just really worried about Julie."

Dawn remained bare naked, as did the other girls. They all stank of body odor, only ever being bathed just before they were called up for a *meeting* with a client. And, when they were washed, it was by a sponge bath or a fire hose. As dirty and cold as Dawn was, all she could do was hold onto the vertical bars of steel and shed a salty tear for her young friend. Her sweat had caked on her skin, making it feel oily and rough. Dawn felt sick and weak, but her own problems paled in comparison to the heart she still had for the innocent. She thought about Proverbs 31:8, which calls us to defend the defenseless.

"I'm so sorry," Stacey offered an olive branch, seeing the immense agony that Dawn was in. "I know how close you are to Julie. She really loves you. You're the sun and moon to her."

"These human traffickers are no better than these humans who enjoy hunting and aborting God's creation. If I ever get my fucking strength back, I will make them all pay. I swear it," Dawn said, as the tears washed down her face, despite her efforts to keep them caged and concealed.

Dawn remembered one of the times when Julie tried to make her laugh. She had told Dawn that they could escape, if they could only quit being stuck in traffic. This was, of course, an attempt to make fun of the sex traffickers who were tormenting and persecuting them. Julie was immature in some ways, while notably insightful in others. Dawn missed her and feared for her.

Sha Na Na's rendition of the song, *Blue Moon*, played on a loop, loudly and exclusively in Dawn's troubled mind. As she firmly held her head, trying desperately to shake out the repeating tune, she kept seeing upsetting visions of Julie dancing provocatively for her arousal. Dawn hated herself for thinking these uninvited and inappropriate thoughts, as they were mentally corrupting her motherly feelings for the youthful innocent. Dawn was psychologically damaged and she knew it all too well, which meant she wasn't a crackpot or a nutcase. They say that crazy people don't know they're crazy, and she was most definitely aware of her illness. Dawn didn't receive delight or ecstasy from harming others, so she wasn't a sociopath or a psychopath. However, she was patently losing her mind and indisputably losing her willpower.

Dawn reached back and furiously scratched her ass, feeling a wicked itch that was relentless and ruthless. As she did this, Cheri was endowed and burdened with the same itch, as if they were both being viciously bitten by a diabolical army of fleas. Cheri lifted her butt off her seat and scratched her wider but equally yummy ass. The difference was, Cheri wound up with her hand coated and covered in blue blood. Though this greatly alarmed the Cambion temptress, it would have comforted her to know that she was on the same wavelength as Dawn.

"What the fuck?!" Cheri said aloud, as she marveled at her blue hand, while continuing to use her clean hand to cruise haphazardly down the never-ending freeway.

The pink-haired misfit considered pulling over and cleaning herself up, but she was more afraid to stop and waste any more time on herself. She was considerably freaked out by the blue fluid that she had dug out of her ass crack, but felt a grievous and dire need to keep driving. Even though it bothered her that this mystery solution was staining the seat cushion underneath her, she could telepathically sense that time was of the utmost importance and quickly running out.

Wolf didn't notice Cheri's crisis, as he was distracted and preoccupied in the back of the Van. He was surrounded by spirits that only his wolf senses could see and hear. Linda was among these, and was wailing at Wolf while sitting in front of him, as if she was desperately trying to tell him something. He could see the fearful and urgent dilemma in Linda's eyes, which woke him up to the critical condition of Dawn's apparent circumstance. This was the first occasion where Linda had appeared to anyone but Dawn, and this time it wasn't because Dawn was about to kill someone. Wolf knew that Dawn must be in a real fix, and it frustrated him to no end that her banshee-mother never spoke…even in moments like this where Dawn was in immediate danger.

"We have to keep moving," Cheri said. "We don't have time to dilly-dally," she declared, as she held her tired eyes open the best she could, and conveniently overlooked the fact that she had turned around multiple times, unable to commit to a cardinal point.

As much driving as Cheri had done, they hadn't covered much ground, as Cheri…much like Dawn…was driving herself insane. Cheri may as well have been driving them up the walls of a giant hamster wheel.

Aside from Linda accosting Wolf, there were other spirits inside and around that Van, including an Italian maiden named, Talia Simonet, who glowed with the moonlight and wore a rosary around her neck. Cheri had more support than she would ever know, as many spirits were fond of Dawn's pummeled but pure heart.

Talia just looked at Wolf, staring into his eyes and leading him to stare into hers. She, unlike Linda, said all she had to say without a sound. Wolf felt chills crawl up his spine, as he saw the horror in Talia's eyes. Though this scared him, he knew that Talia wasn't a threat, but that she was there as more of an omen. He could see the despair and distress in her eyes, and the genuine concern that Talia had, not only for Dawn, but for him.

AUGUST 6, 1979
CORN MOON

Selene, also known as, *Mene* (when she appears in male form), is the sister of Helios (the Sun) and is often found flirting and frolicking with Diana (a fellow moon goddess). Selene often pursued romantic liaisons with this Roman huntress, as well as countless human men. Selene is a heartless whore, who has no intention or interest in becoming emotionally attached to any of her playmates. This slutty deity eventually hooked up with a teenage shepherd named, Endymion, who distracted her enough to shirk her nightly duty of guiding the moon through the skies. The other Greek gods noticed Selene's strange behavior, and that her chariot was often missing from its heavenly corral.

Night after night, Selene visited the naïve youth, slipping into his bed and creeping into his dreams. She became abnormally pale from her nightly rendezvous, and her sins eventually came to bite her in the ass. Zeus became enraged and stepped in to intervene, giving Endymion the choice of instant death or eternal youth. There was a stipulation, however, to the latter option. If he chose eternal youth, it would come with eternal sleep, meaning though he'd never age, he would never have the chance to enjoy his immortality. It is said that Endymion then became known as, *Iduna*, that he still sleeps to this day, lives in a Carian cave on *Mount Latmos*, and that Selene still visits and has intercourse with him.

While she lays with her snoozing shepherd, the moon fades away until it is totally gone. When Selene returns to her duties, the moon begins to grow again until it reaches Full mass. Even though Endymion only sees his moon goddess in his dreams, legend has it that she has borne him fifty beautiful daughters. Endymion symbolizes the subconscious, the imagination, and the magical influence caused by the phases of the moon. As Endymion bears daughters with Selene in his slumber, so are we fertilized with creative ideas during our receptive resting periods, be it in dreams, daydreams, visions, or meditation.

As Cheri sleeps in her van, she dreams that she is visited by a moon goddess. Selene appears to be wearing a shiny, silver crown and a glittery, silver bounce-back tunic. The crown resembles something from medieval times. The tunic features a round neckline, long sleeves, a double slit front with lattice detailing, an invisible back zipper, and a flattering curve-hugging fit. Selene hands Cheri thirty cherries, which all turn black as soon as they make contact with Cheri's palm.

Cheri then looks up to see Selene joined by a woman who wore a flowing blue robe, a pearl necklace, a white shell on her back, and butterfly wings. Her name was, Mezratu, and she held a rabbit in her hands that she called, Ostarra. This rabbit had a crescent-shaped nose and smelled like pulque beer. While Cheri watched in horror, Mezratu stabbed the bunny with her abnormally long and lethal fingernails, which caused the white rabbit to explode. However, instead of blood rushing out of this small animal, it was salt water.

As this salt water splashed in Cheri's face, she turned around to see another woman, named Hecate, who was silver-footed. None of these women spoke, but Cheri somehow still managed to identify them.

Cheri suddenly snapped out of her bad dream, and as she abruptly awoke, she found herself holding a silver disk in her hands, which had a human face in its center.

"Mama Quilla?" the disk face asked, significantly freaking her out. When she didn't answer, the spooky disk asked again. "Mama Cocha?" Cheri dropped the disk, which made a loud horn noise as it smacked against the ground, which was also made of silver.

Cheri came out of her dream again, this time for real, only to find that she had fallen asleep at the wheel. She was driving on the wrong side of the road and an obnoxious semi-truck was honking at her, stubbornly unwilling to be the one to maneuver. Cheri immediately panicked and instinctively swerved out of his way. The belligerent driver flicked her off, as he aggressively brushed passed her. After pulling over on the side of the highway, she saw an esoteric duplicate of herself sitting in the passenger's seat. It was an ectoplasm version of herself, but was herself nonetheless.

"Don't mind our thoughts," she said to Cheri. "The Devil can mess with our mind, but can't touch our hearts…unless we let him." With that, the metaphysical mirage vanished, as if being erased or never there. Did Cheri just experience an optical illusion or a deranged hallucination? Could she ever be any good for Dawn, if she was crazy herself?

SEPTEMBER 6, 1979
WINE MOON

Cheri continues to drive, without having the slightest clue of their desired destination, hoping that the powers of luck and chance might guide them in the right direction. As she and Wolf gaze up at the lunar eclipse, careful to not miss a moment's glimpse, her head suddenly feels heavy and falls back. Her eyes roll into her skull, and she blinks relentlessly as if her lids were having a seizure. Wolf gets spooked as he witnesses her body mutate into a cloud of fine mist. Within a matter of seconds, the bohemian Cheri disappears and transcendentally teleports to where Dawn is. Cheri had become a lucid dream, as this was far beyond a simple out-of-body-experience. She then literally enters Dawn through her vaginal cavity and becomes part of her paranormal subconscious, assuming control and turning her nightmare into Dawn's wet dream. As all this takes place, Cheri somehow continues to drive her Van as if she were awake and alert.

Hours later, Cheri returns to Wolf, back in her anatomic shape, with the new ability to psychically communicate with Dawn. They could now telepathically read each other's thoughts, and Cheri therefore no longer had to wonder or guess where Dawn was being held captive. When Dawn's terminus is revealed to Cheri, through ESP, she promptly turns her Van around and heads toward the *City by the Bay*, also known as, *Fog City*. She's no longer scatter-brained, but focused on the yellow-brick road ahead of her, which is finally paved and irradiated. While Cheri was still inside Dawn, both women could hear the 1967 song, *San Francisco*, but it wasn't Scott McKenzie providing the vocals, but rather them doing their own cover. They weren't actually singing, but they saw themselves performing the song in their heads and did so in beautiful harmony.

Since it had been confirmed that Julie had in fact been murdered by one of the prestigious clients, Dawn began thinking hard about her own mortality. Joy's curse, which Dawn was still oblivious to, had given no sign of ever leaving her, and she was only getting sicker and weaker by the day. Dawn knew she may never see Wolf or Cheri again, and that scared her. Not only was she heartbroken, but she was helpless in aiding her new friends in her new nightmare. She genuinely cared for these girls, and had especially grown to care for Julie. Now, Julie had been snuffed from her life and taken away from her, like everyone else she had ever given her love to. Dawn wasn't good for anyone, and now it looked like her time was nearly up.

"What's the matter?" Claire asked. "You look like you're hung up on a dude?"

"It's more like she's hung up on me," Dawn admitted openly, while blatantly denying that it was mutual.

"She?" Stacey asked.

"Damn. You're nutty," Karen said.

"I think that's neato," Teri lied, pretending that she admired her bisexuality. "Good for you, lesbo."

"I'm afraid," Dawn confessed. "I'm scared shitless that I'm going to burn in Hell for what I've done."

"I don't know what you've done," Karen said, "but, according to the Word of God, all sin is equal in the Lord's eyes."

"That's actually not Biblical at all. I realize that this is what ministers like to convince people, but it's not supported by Scripture. The Christian church tells us that *all sin is equal* and that *good deeds don't get us into Heaven*, but both of these statements plainly contradict the passage in Romans 2:6-11."

"You speak like you're a deacon or something?" Karen expressed, insulted that Dawn was correcting her on this.

"Something," Dawn answered simply but sincerely. Dawn saw the disillusioned look in Karen's eyes, as if she had burst a reality bubble in her that she wasn't prepared for in the slightest. "One of the few things they tell you in church, that's actually accurate, is that blasphemy of the Holy Spirit is the only unforgivable sin. What's scary about this, however, is that this passage is one of the many parts of the Bible that is extremely vague. None of us really know what blasphemy of the Holy Spirit is, short of saying those actual words in hateful disrespect. But, yeah...most of what preachers tell you in church is their own biased opinion or bold interpretation of the Gospel, not the actual Gospel."

"Have you ever blasphemed the Holy Ghost?" Stacy asked the educated preacher's daughter.

"Hell, no," Dawn answered quickly and truthfully. "I might be a raving lunatic, but I'm not stupid. No, I would never do that."

"But, you're pretty confident that you'll wind up in Hell anyway?" Stacy asked.

"In certain ways, I'm already there. But, yes, I'm terrified that I'll end up there after I die," she admitted. "I'm pretty sure that God hates me. He's made that painfully clear. All the signs point to that being the case."

Dawn's friends talk amongst themselves, reminding each other how the early Christians of the Bible were tortured and persecuted, while later Christians burned alleged heretics at the stake. They found it unsettling how, throughout history, Christians had turned from such tenderhearted believers to covetous, biased, inhuman hypocrites. None of the girls were perfect, but they took pride in the fact that they were authentic and had their hearts in the right place.

As they continued to vent over their collective intolerance of evil, Dawn gently shut her eyes in meditation. She took a deep breath, slowly exhaled, and imagined that she was outside in an open field, laying under the soothing moonlight. Dawn, in their shared cell, could hear Nikolas's voice again, as he ridiculed her for being weak, even though her infirmity wasn't her own doing. His objective was to try and tear her down to the point of self-destruction, or at least that's how it appeared.

"We don't waste our kindness on ingrates or weaklings. It's a greater crime to keep people alive who are never going to be productive, who drain our resources, and create a stagnant world. We are not obliged to save the frail and feeble. Christians seek to help the weak, not because they care, but because it boosts their pomposity. Churches derive pleasure from going to places like Haiti and Uganda, because it makes them look good. Nobody really cares about anybody, including your Lord," Nikolas insisted. "So, why should you? You cared for Julie, and now God has eliminated her. You couldn't save her, just like you couldn't save Reuben or your son. Everything you touch, and everyone who touches you, turns to shit. You're no good to anyone, Dawn; not even to yourself."

The steroid-pumped, *Boner*, came to visit Dawn again, but this time to rub it in her face about Julie.

"It's a shame what happened to your psychotic friend, isn't it?" he said, grinning with perverse pride and audacity. "What was her name again? Julie? Yeah, she was a nutcase, wasn't she? Seeing things that weren't there, and all. If only she had had a bit more foresight, and could see that I was setting her up with a convicted child killer."

Dawn's ears perked up, as she heard him practically confess to being the one responsible for Julie's untimely demise.

"If it's any consolation, I heard that the preferred client made her death as painful as possible. She went screaming, I'm told. They told me that she was crying for you, Dawn. How pathetic is that? Apparently, she kept calling out your name over and over again. How hilarious is that? I'll tell you, I sure enjoyed it," he boasted joyfully, entertained by the look of unadulterated anguish on Dawn's face.

As weak and frail as Dawn was, she felt a burst of energy overcome her body. She could feel the hate coarse through her veins, as she stared at the giant-sized, Middle Eastern bully. "You, son of a bitch! I'll kill you, mother fucker! I'll fucking kill you!! You're dead!! You hear me, asshole?! You're fucking dead!!" she yelled, as she quickly got up off the floor and hurled herself, like a tomahawk, against the chilled steel. As she violently collided with the vertical bars, she knocked herself out cold. The other girls quickly came to her aid and wept for their distraught friend, as the Muslim perpetrator laughed in twisted amusement.

While Dawn was once again lost in the darkness, she heard the Supertramp song, *Goodbye Stranger*, playing exclusively in her head. As she listened to the private concert and Roger Hodgson's appropriate lyrics, her eyes filled up with salty tears for Julie and her abused heart was becoming more hardened, numb, and overflowing with unfiltered, concentrated animosity.

While her friends cried for and over Dawn, two gruesome ghouls appeared in their cell. Boner couldn't see them, but the girls could. Frightened for their lives, they backed away and let this pair of blood-curdling phantoms approach and kneel before Dawn's limp body. These two manifestations were ghastly in appearance, but their visit was one of charity and clemency.

"We are Asena and Ashina," they introduced themselves, using what seemed to be a Turkish accent. They looked like abominable snowmen, except they were female and had the fangs, claws, and ears of a werewolf. "Dawn's body collapsed because it is cursed, and wasn't capable of handling the adrenaline that surged through her or the blunt collision that knocked her out. We are shamans from beyond, who have come to nurse her back to health. We cannot lift the curse, but we can keep her from dying. Our help, however, is a one-time deal."

Asena laid her hands on Dawn's chest, while Ashina touched her bloody head. The girls were too afraid to verbally address the creatures, so they just nodded and gave the visitors space. Boner didn't even notice this strange behavior, as he was too focused on jerking off and laughing at Dawn's breakdown. Somehow, Dawn was resuscitated and her bashed-in head was healed.

SEPTEMBER 24, 1980
FULL MOON
RESCUE DAWN

Dawn's hypertrichosis had started to produce more extra body hair, not just around her pubic region, but everywhere. She was transforming into somewhat of a Lycan, looking more and more like her condition wasn't all in her head.

Dawn couldn't articulate or analyze the love connection she had, and continues to have, with her pygophiliac boyfriend. She missed Reuben so deeply, that it physically hurt. *Love* wasn't a big enough word for how she felt, and would always feel, for him. The only silver lining in her endless chain of traumatic adversity was her feelings for Cheri and Wolf. Reuben and their son had been taken from her, neither of which were her fault. She turned her back on her dear companions, and she did deserve blame and accountability for that. Leaving Wolf and Cheri tormented her almost as much as living without Reuben. She looks up at the ceiling to their cell and howls in excruciating pain, while the other girls latch onto her as if they never wanted to let go.

The *Mr. Crowley* song is playing in the dungeon, just to annoy the female prisoners and make them feel more uneasy. The ominous tune is playing on an endless loop, while the girls walk around in a melancholic circle, as if playing musical chairs without the chairs. As Ozzy Osbourne's voice reverberates throughout the clandestine lair, Dawn and her friends look like zombies as they sluggishly move to the Metal music. It was almost the stroke of midnight, and the moon was distinctively peculiar that night. The full moon had two crescent moons on either side of it, as if their backs were leaning against the center moon.

"You're a long way from the reservation, honey," one of the thuggish brutes joked, as he threw a bowl of expired dog food at Dawn's face.

The red dwarf appeared again, this time while Dawn was still awake. The other girls didn't appear to see him, which made her wonder if she was just daydreaming. The malicious guards ridiculed and mocked her, relishing how she looked with wet dog chow on her face. Dawn, however, failed to hear their laughter or even acknowledge the assault, as she was too distracted by the sinister phantasm that she, and only she, could see.

"Who are you?" she asked him, demanding to know his name.

"Nain Rouge," he answered.

"What do you want from me?" she asked, now that he was finally answering her and acknowledging her questions.

"Feu follet," he replied, still refusing to communicate with her in a way that she could understand, knowing full well that she didn't know any French.

"Feu follet?" she repeated in the form of a question.

"Ta mort," he said, grinning slyly from ear to ear.

Cheri finally reaches her destination of San Francisco, but as she does, her journey takes a whole new turn. A wormhole appears directly in front of her, just as her Van crosses over the California state line. Before she can do anything about it or even process what she's seeing before her, she drives them right through it.

This isn't like being caught in the middle of a tornado, but instead was no more complicated than walking through a door. As soon as they came out on the other side, a newspaper conveniently blew onto their windshield. Cheri hit the brakes and stopped the van. She gets out and finds the newspaper, which was now laying on the asphalt of a parking lot.

"Well, what do you know?" she said aloud to herself, as she read the date on the paper. "Son of a bitch."

Rather than be propelled to a parallel universe, the portal served as a time warp. Cheri and Wolf find themselves losing an entire year, in the blink of an eye. On the positive side, not only does this wormhole carry them a full year into the future, but it takes Cheri's van to the precise place they need to be. She is shocked to discover that the location of Dawn's captivity is none other than a battered women's shelter.

"Of course," she said aloud, as she parked her Van. "It would be something like this," she added, shaking her head. "Well, do you want to come, Wolf?"

Wolf looked at her with his head cocked to the side, as if to convey to her that this was a stupid question.

"Well, alright then," she said, scratching the top of Wolf's head. "Let's kick some ass and go get our Dawn back."

Wolf growled and snarled to let Cheri know that he was beyond ready. They walked up to the doors, only to find that they were heavily constructed and secured.

"Well, shit, Wolf. It looks like they have this place locked up like *Fort Knox*. I guess that makes sense though, huh?"

Wolf just looked up at her and whimpered, as he was as discouraged as she was about not being able to break in. Cheri would have busted her way through, but she wasn't blessed with the hidden muscle that Dawn had. She could have set the doors on fire, but not without the arson causing too much attention. Cheri did, however, have other ideas at her disposal. She and Wolf hid behind a dumpster, which was off to the side of the lot, and waited patiently for someone to either come out or go in. After staking the place out for about an hour, they finally spot a woman approaching the door. As she's taking out her keys to let herself in, Cheri taps her on the shoulder. Turning around, the woman sees Wolf, who is bearing his teeth and looking at her like she's an appetizer. The startled woman quickly fidgets with her keys, trying to find the right one, but in her nervousness, she drops them on the ground. Cheri sticks her hand out in front of her and wiggles her fingers, using telekinesis to bring the keys up to her palm. The employed woman watches this happen, and freaks out in a panic.

"Jesus Christ!" she screams, backing up against the doors and placing her hands against the bulletproof glass, as if doing this will somehow magically protect her from inevitable harm. "Who are you? What do you want?"

"This is a women's shelter, isn't it?" Cheri asked, rhetorically. "Shelter me."

"Are y-you an abused w-wife?" the stuttering lady asked, trying desperately to catch her breath.

"Well, something tells me you people know a lot about abuse, don't you?" Cheri said, as she stared into the woman's eyes and could see the dark secrets that she was keeping. "This place is a front, isn't it? You're destroying girls underneath this piece-of-shit property, aren't you?"

"I don't know what you're talking about?" the woman lied, trying to save herself by denying the truth that was clearly exposed.

"Oh, I think you do. I think you're holding our friend down there, which is unacceptable and unforgiveable," Cheri said, as the scared lady saw her eyes literally turn to flame for just a millisecond. She saw how furious Cheri was, and saw her open mouth drool saliva that sizzled when it struck the ground.

"Please, don't hurt me," the woman pleaded, realizing that she was dealing with something supernatural. "I'll do anything you want," she begged, while Cheri had to keep her hand on Wolf's cold nose, just to stop him from leaping on the woman and ripping her to shreds.

"First," Cheri began, "you're going to show me which key opens these doors, and then you're going to take us where we want to go. Do what I tell you, and we just might let you live," she fibbed, having no intention on letting her or anybody else walk away from this despicable den of iniquity.

When Cheri and Wolf find Dawn, she and the other girls wreak of feces, body odor, and urine, are covered in bruises, and are visibly dehydrated and malnourished. Though they had a toilet in their cell, they were never provided with any toiletries or ways to clean themselves. The lovestruck Cheri stretches out her arm and magically materializes a bullwhip in her hand. The whip is made of fire and has a triangular tip, like a devil's tail. Throwing her arm back, she mercilessly and aggressively takes out her unhinged wrath on the slave traders for daring to subject Dawn to such atrocities. She loses both her short temper and her disturbed mind as she violently assassinates each and every one of the human traffickers, execution style.

Boner sees what's happening and starts to run towards Cheri with fury and indignation, but is quickly stopped short by her whip, which catches him around the neck and instantly incinerates his skull.

"Noooo!!" Dawn shouts, as she sees this happen. Though she is grateful to Cheri for coming to her rescue, she is both devastated and disappointed to see her take out Boner. This was something that Dawn had been longing to do herself, on her own, for so many reasons.

While Wolf continues to do his part in contributing to the massacre, Cheri uses her fiery bullwhip to open the six cells that are holding female victims, beginning with the one holding Dawn and her friends. Cheri's devilish whip slices right through the iron bars and the locks that hold them. Dawn takes a handful of the blood spatter and applies it on her face like war paint, before joining in on the fun, killing the last two traffickers with her bare hands. She even uses her jaws to scalp both of them, which she then proudly holds above her head and yells out a victory cheer in her native tongue.

Just then, an oblivious Muslim woman casually enters the room, who was the obedient wife of the steroid-pumped goon that had tormented Dawn for the duration of her forced stay. The woman strutted, in her pride and prejudice, wearing clothes that made it clear that she had been born with a silver spoon in her mouth. Dawn miraculously and instinctively leaps on Boner's widow, pinning the rich reprobate to the ground. Dawn had gone completely bananas, by this point, and chose this particularly offensive individual to go ape-shit on.

"I've had enough!!" Dawn screamed, almost incoherently, as white saliva foamed from the corners of her mouth. "How the fuck can you embrace such a heinous religion?! You like how Islam endorses genital mutilation?! Have you done that to your daughter yet?!" she asked the thug's widow, hypothetically, not knowing if she and *Boner* even had any children. "How about you? Did that ever happen to you?! Let's see, shall we?" Dawn's sweet and sensual voice had suddenly become deep and dark.

Dawn used her razor-sharp claws to slice and dice through the consort's heavy layers of fabric, until she had carved a path to the woman's bushy, pubic region. Shoving her hand inside the missus's humid vagina, she continued reaching until grabbing hold of her cervix. Yanking it out of her, she threw the destroyed body part off to the side, as the mutilated Arab woman screamed in indescribable agony and unnerving terror. Dawn's strength was nonexistent, but she refused to pass on this opportunity to maul and mar this woman, especially since Cheri had already disposed of the one responsible for Julie's ultimate and unfortunate doom.

"Oh, wait," Dawn said, in second thought, "that's right. You mutilate those little girls, so they can never experience pleasure. Sorry, I removed the wrong piece." With that, Dawn grabbed the top of the woman's pussy and brutally ripped off her clitoris. She then held it up in front of the woman's face, so she could see it, as she slowly but surely bled to death.

"Qabul," the woman said softly, before closing her eyes forever. Once the woman passed out from shock, Dawn inserted the Muslim's bloody, vaginal flesh into the woman's mouth, and then got up from off of her.

The other girls were frozen in horror, having watched Dawn rip Boner's wife to shreds and tearing off each limb as if they were rotisserie chicken legs. They saw their friend's blue eyes turn pitch black and her beautiful brown hair turn snow white. Dawn's progressive transformation, that was once only visible to her, had escalated and graduated to public perception.

"Holy fuck," the Bible-loving Karen said, in total shock.

"The Egyptians believe in a god they call, *Khepera*, who they claim is a moon god of transformation. They say he has the head of a scarab," Claire shared her book knowledge.

"Those Egyptians sure are intelligent, aren't they? They definitely got the gender right and the beetle part right," Teri noted sarcastically, as Dawn was anything but those things.

"Actually, the Navajo call her, *Estsanatlehi*," Dawn corrects, smiling again for the first time in a long time, and showing off her blood-stained teeth.

As the neurotic Cherokee begins to step away from the dismembered Muslim, she looks back at the butchered heathen, and says, under her breath, "Damn, you crazy cats aren't playing with a full deck, are you?" She then looks back at her shaken cellmates, leaving them to wonder if Dawn was talking to them or the demolished Muslim woman on the floor.

Dawn was surging with energy, as her heightened senses and supernatural strength were once again rushing through her veins. Her body, however, was still burdened with Joy's hex, and therefore was unequipped to handle the power that was trying to return to her. Immediately after she says this, Dawn feels herself slipping into a cataleptic condition. She collapses, having used more energy than she had to help Cheri out with the vengeful slaughter. Dawn had only been able to do what she did, from the rush of hatred that demanded retribution, but it had taken its toll on her. Her emotional and hostile outburst had cost her dearly, as her infirm body was not capable of handling such rage or mending her wounds. She belly-flopped on the ground, while Cheri cried out in hysterical concern. Dawn wasn't breathing.

Wolf witnessed Dawn go bonkers and now lay limp on the floor. Cheri knelt at her side, weeping over her, afraid that their rescue had been too little too late. Wolf intuitively and instinctively stepped up to her other side, that Cheri wasn't occupying. As Dawn lied there on the brink of death, she slowly opened her eyes and saw Reuben's eyes in Wolf's. She knew she was close to the end, and didn't know if what she was seeing was a delusional trance or something real, but her dead lover seemed to be in harmony with her furry friend, as if they had both come to save her together. Cheri couldn't pinpoint Joy's sadistic hex in Dawn's bloodstream, but Wolf detected the infection right off the bat, as if it outlined her figure. Like a wise shaman who knew that only he could help her, Wolf leaned in towards Dawn's pretty neck.

"I call on the great spirit, Wakan Tanka," a voice said out of nowhere, which resembled the late Reuben, but sounded slightly different and more animalistic.

Wolf knew that it would be risky to bite her, since she was so vulnerable and fragile, but he had no choice. He begged God to lift the damaging hex from Dawn's soul and place it on his own. He silently repeated this interceding mantra ten times, willing to damn himself if it was the only way to save his dear companion. Wolf chomped down on her shoulder, and as he left his fangs in her, he sucked out the curse from her poisoned blood. He could see that she was too frail and weak, and feared that his bite might inadvertently kill her, but he had to try. Once Wolf felt that he had absorbed the demon's toxin, the enlightened guardian bowed his head and shut his eyes in solemn prayer. The mystical transference was successful and the trickster's curse was expelled from Dawn's body, but was now hurting the willing sin-eater.

Moments later, a healing wave magically swept over and blanketed her complete being. Dawn's werewolf powers had returned, her shoulder had healed, and she had fully recovered. She had completely regenerated and now felt stronger than ever. Cheri helped her sit up, even though Dawn needed no assistance. When Dawn had collected herself and processed her surroundings, she noticed that Wolf's head was resting motionless on her lap. She put her hand under his nose, feeling no breath or warmth. He was gone, just like Reuben and just like Donnie. Joy's curse had left, but tragically at the expense of her endearing friend.

"He saved your life," Cheri said, sniffling, as her chin trembled and her heart ached. "He gave his life for yours," she added, amazed and awed with how he had adored her so.

Dawn wanted to weep with Cheri, over the tragic loss of her dearly departed ally, but she found herself numb to the emotions she knew she felt inside. Wolf's selfless sacrifice had been too much, and had pushed her over the edge. Dawn was now completely gone and she herself had died in every way but physically. Joy's destructive hex had been too much for Wolf to bear or carry, as he did not share Dawn's resistant and resilient gift of lycanthropy.

The two estranged lovers immediately held an emotional funeral for Wolf, where they both said goodbye to their irreplaceable and tenderhearted friend.

"Do you think he'll go to Heaven?" Dawn asked, finally blubbering in streaming sadness.

"Honey, I don't know?" Cheri admitted honestly. "I would hope so, but I don't know if animals are welcomed into Heaven or not? I don't know God's policy on that?"

"I am an animal," Dawn told her pink-haired lover, "or at least I can be," she added, meaning both *sexually wild* and *capable of extreme violence*.

Dawn and Cheri had freed the other sex slaves, at least the ones who hadn't already been sold and whisked away to God knows where. A few of the girls wanted to stay with Dawn, which was touching and tear-jerking, but just not possible. Dawn worried about what would become of them, since setting them free was very much like taking a domesticated pet (that had always been pampered and protected) and dropping it off in the middle of the jungle, expecting it to suddenly fend for itself.

The Scripture verses of Mark 5:11-13 & Matthew 8:28-34 came to Dawn's memory as a reminder that animals have more common sense than most humans. She also remembered all the verses in the Bible that compare Jesus to different animals, and describe angels as having animal-like features and traits. She felt confident that Wolf made it to Heaven, as it wouldn't make any sense otherwise. Believing that Wolf was in Heaven, along with Reuben and Donnie, was the only thing that offered her any comfort or serenity. Wolf had selflessly sacrificed himself so that Dawn would be safe and restored. Dawn felt her heart warm as she thought of her feral friend, who had displayed more love and kindness towards her than most homo sapiens had.

"Thank you, Wolf," she whispered to herself, under her breath, as she got choked up over her great loss. "I will always love you and never forget you. Thank you for my life and for your friendship."

Three hours later…

"I'm sorry," Dawn apologized.

"For what?" Cheri asked, confused.

"I know I'm a drag, not a blessing."

Cheri saw that Dawn's pep had completely dissipated into nothingness. "Don't be silly," she told Dawn. "You're not a burden. I like looking after you."

Something was different about Dawn, and Cheri noticed. Her words of reassurance appeared to have little to zero effect, and it made Cheri feel helpless. She sensed that something fishy must've went on behind the closed doors of the slave dungeon that she had found

Dawn in. Dawn wasn't telling her something, and not even a pricey makeover with lipstick, blush, and long fake eyelashes, was going to repair whatever she was hiding. They had left the underground syndicate in a pool of poetic justice, which the incompetent, local authorities wouldn't catch wind of for several weeks. Dawn was finding it harder than ever to resist or deny her violent impulses, and it scared her beyond words. She loved Cheri, and was worried that she couldn't trust herself not to harm her. The line between right and wrong, deliberate and unintentional, had become blurred. She had lost so much, having such vital pieces of her heart ripped away, and now feared that she'd hurt the one love she had left.

The song, *Take The Long Way Home*, by Supertramp, plays over the radio, while Dawn rests in the back after crying herself to sleep. She's snuggling with a stuffed wolf that Cheri had bought from a toy store, while she and Wolf had been in Wyoming. Dawn loved her present, but because of the traumatic experiences with the sex traffickers, it resurfaced some repressed memories that she would have preferred remained buried. Dawn appeared to have a gentle disposition in spite the circumstances, but her calmness was a cover for her inconsolable grief, which was eating away at her and leading her down a slippery slope of self-destruction. Dawn imagined herself being taken back to Cheri's hip pad and it quite honestly didn't appeal to her, but she decided she would rather take that to her grave than ever admit that to Cheri.

"Dawn, I don't know if you're awake back there, but, if you are…please hear me. I'm so sorry, sweetheart. I chased you through four states because I've had a change of heart. You are my heart, baby girl. I love you, Dawn, and I hope you can forgive me and give us a second chance. I know I don't deserve it, but I promise you won't regret it." Looking in her rearview mirror, Cheri noticed a distance in Dawn's eyes and mistook this to be something about her or their fractured relationship, but the truth was, Cheri wasn't in the doghouse. Dawn had just lost her wish and will to go on. "I'm sorry that it took so long to find you, baby. I'm so sorry, Dawn."

While they were traveling through the Centennial state, they stopped at a few casinos in the historic gambling towns of *Black Hawk* and *Central City*. Here, they found alcoholic beverages to be dirt-cheap and wealthy snobs who were eager to lose their money. Dawn caught herself staring aimlessly at a jukebox menu, where she related a bit too well to several of the available songs by Bob Seger & The Silver Bullet Band. *Till it Shines*, *Looking Back*, *Sunburst*, *Sunspot Baby*, *Ship of Fools*, *Maybe Today*, *Black Night*, *Sailing Nights* and *Fine Memory* were among the tracks to choose from.

They also stopped at a Sasquatch Outpost in Bailey, CO. Cheri made the lethargic Dawn get up and come inside with her, so she could stretch her legs and get the blood flowing through her veins. As soon as they walked in the door of the fandom establishment, all eyes immediately turned on Dawn. The customers and employees both looked at Dawn as if she was a freak. They couldn't visually see her werewolf traits, but many could feel her aura, which was what scared them stiff. These people were already believers in the supernatural, but they hadn't anticipated seeing anything like Dawn that day, or ever.

Dawn found a comic book about *Bigfoot*, while browsing the different racks and tables of geeky goodies. There were also *Scratch N' Sniff* stickers that caught her attention. She reached up and felt her mouthful of teeth, surprised to find that the ones she had lost…or rather been booted out of her…had all grown back. One middle-aged man, in particular, was courageous enough to approach the alluring, but ominous, young woman. The underwear he was wearing was marked in *Sharpie,* by his mother, who still wrote his name is his briefs.

"You look like you came straight from the pages of *Dungeons & Dragons*," he said, meaning it as a high compliment and fascinated by her very presence.

This made Dawn significantly uncomfortable, as she didn't want such attention from strangers, particularly of the male persuasion. She was bogged down with manic depression, but still noticed their ogles and stares. Dawn wasn't comfortable in her own skin anymore, and certainly wasn't comfortable being drooled over. Cheri also perceived their unwelcomed, dirty looks, and didn't hesitate to reciprocate them. Cheri was over protective of Dawn and was determined to not lose her twice. Both her eyes were fixed on Dawn, and that's where they would remain.

People watched, in cruel judgment, until the two rug munchers stepped out and returned to Cheri's van. When they got back on the road, Cheri turned and looked at Dawn, who still refused to sit up front with her. She insisted on riding in the back, where Wolf used to lay. Cheri saw the redness on Dawn's face and could tell that she was getting worse, not better. Joy's curse had been lifted, but Dawn was clearly broken beyond repair. The loss of her faithful and furry friend had pushed her over the cliff's edge, and there was no coming back. Cheri's initial intention was to drive them home to her apartment in Texas, but she thought better of it and realized that her plan would only bring Dawn back to an environment that would cater to her painful memories. She needed to whisk Dawn away to an unfamiliar destination, one which bore no negative energy or bad reflection, but allowed room for recovery and healing.

Cheri had French roots in Paris and decided to take Dawn to *The City of Light*, where they could both move on and start over…together. She knew that Dawn needed stability and couldn't handle being a nomad any longer. She needed a fresh ambience, one which would offer peace and remedy. The only question that needed to be considered was how they would afford this elaborate and permanent vacation. She didn't want to bother taking the time to go home and sell everything she owned. Dawn didn't have that much time and Cheri knew the sense of urgency that was in front of them. Cheri couldn't let their relationship sink, and was afraid that she would lose Dawn again if she didn't save the Cherokee beauty from drowning in her own tears. Dawn was hanging on by a thin thread and Cheri knew it. If God wasn't going to cure or help her, then Cheri needed to find a way to mend whatever ailed and crushed her spirit.

Cheri knew that Mathias had been someone who never had financial worries. He died loaded, with more money than he could have spent in ten lifetimes. Cheri pulled over to the side of the highway and put her blinkers on. She gently shut her eyes and meditated on what Mathias once looked like. After nine minutes of this, she could feel her body become his. She reached up to touch her face and felt his instead. She looked at her faux reflection in the rearview mirror, and verified that she had become the late alchemist. She had also acquired his clothes, as part of the charade. She reached inside his coat and then in his front pocket, until she found his fat wallet. Cheri took out the wad of cash he had at the time of his death, and all of his credit cards, of which he had many.

As soon as she had taken what she needed from him, she watched in the mirror as she returned to normal. Because she had briefly been him, she was able to read his thoughts and see inside his decaying head. This postmortem possession had given her access to all of his personal information, including pin numbers and passwords. They had struck the lottery. Every one of Mathias's cards were unlimited, exclusive, and had the highest status. They had it made. Mathias and Joy had been reduced to ash, leaving no evidence that they were dead. There was nobody left to complain and no reason to suspect foul play or fraudulent activity. Before they shelled out for their extravagant trip, Cheri wanted to make one last stop. She was anxious to take Dawn away from it all, but before they left America behind for good, she wanted them to leave on a happy ending.

Cheri switches to wearing her rings on her right hand. It sickened her that Joy's left hand had been decorated with rings too. Cheri asked Dawn about what happened to her during her time being in the hands of the traffickers. Rather than open up about it, Dawn denied that anything had happened, which was the first time she had ever lied to her pink raspberry. Cheri knew that her fabricated story didn't hold any water, but she also could see that Dawn was sinking faster than she could think.

Cheri wanted nothing more than to save her, but she knew that any efforts would wind up being washed away in a landslide.

"I can't compare to Reuben's *Hershey*-bar turds, but I can promise to love you as much as he did," Cheri graphically conveyed, exaggerating to make her point. "In your eyes, he was the perfect specimen and companion. I get that, I really do, but he's gone, baby. I'm not. I will never ask you to stop loving Reuben, but I hope you will love me too, if not just as intensely. When we hook up, I don't know about you, but I see fireworks. Maybe what we have isn't a supernova, like what you and Reuben share, but I think you're the most, Dawn. My feelings for you run deep, sweetheart. Maybe I'm not a gingerbread stud-muffin, but I promise you that I will love you as genuinely as he does. What we have is special, Dawn. Please don't light a match to our fated connection."

Neither Dawn or Cheri knew if their love had been fortuitous, or if it was destined by the stars, but they knew it was meant to be and were going to fight for it until one of them dropped. Dawn and Cheri had both become turncoats, with Cheri renouncing her demonic roots, and Dawn crawling back to the God that she felt so blighted and forsaken by.

Dawn convinces Cheri to let them cash in their stolen funds for a one-way adventure to France, after Cheri manipulates her mind. Cheri, wanting to make her lipstick-lover happy, agreed. Neither of them had passports, but with Cheri's mind-control power, they didn't require the necessary documentation. She knew that Dawn needed a break from the abundance of monsters that sought to steal her joy, even though there was no turning back the clock. Cheri wanted to be sensitive to the devastating and detrimental trauma that Dawn had suffered, but she also missed her dollish figure and hoped that their relocating to Paris might open Dawn up again to letting them fool around.

The pink-haired Cambion had never seen Australia's *Down Under*, but wished that their moon goddess of erotic dreams, *Gidja*, would somehow bewitch Dawn on her behalf. Sex wasn't the most important thing to Cheri, but that didn't change the fact that she was addicted to Dawn. It was impossible not to miss scoring with her intoxicating, perfect-10 body. When Cheri heard songs like Peter McCann's, *Do You Wanna Make Love*, it only reminded her of that.

Cheri cruises down the road with her newly-frigid ladylove, looking for a way to leave their mark on America before saying their final farewell. It was a soggy night, with a mist that swirled and teetered on developing into light rain. They had been motoring on an exceptionally desolate stretch of road that was engulfed by wide-open, scrubby ranch land. The area was sparsely freckled with humble homes and independent businesses. Because of the inclement weather, Cheri had slowed down to under 10mph, not getting much help from the windshield wipers. It was here when Cheri and Dawn both felt a sharp pain in their temples. It was as if their brain waves were attached, mutually sharing the cerebral attack. This neurological assault was coming from uninvited company.

Even though the Van wasn't going fast, it began to shake and shimmy. Cheri feared that their tires would blow out, but it was a sinister presence instead of a transmission issue. Three young people ambled towards their slow-moving van, without showing any intimidation or trepidation. Cheri and Dawn both saw these strangers, instantly feeling an uneasiness that made their skin crawl. These three were all wearing matching uniforms, which consisted of dark-colored, preppy sweaters. They walked directly towards them, while hanging their heads, as if they weren't bothered or dissuaded by the danger of being run over. Cheri and Dawn looked at one another and silently agreed that there was something odd about this. One of the three, now seen clearly in the headlight beams, looked up and pointed directly at Dawn. This boy's skin was albino and his perplexing eyes were solid black. The ensuing chill ran down Cheri's spine before she put pedal to metal and sped off. These three young men, though impeccably dressed, were shrouded with turpitude. Dawn looked out the window, as they left the scary trio in the dust.

OCTOBER 13, 1980
BLOOD MOON

Dawn sings karaoke to the Johnny Mercer song, *Moon River*, first softly, then boldly. She receives lecherous looks from the eerie crowd of human vipers. The man playing the piano, turns to look at her and she sees that half of his face is horribly disfigured. Yet, he smiles gleefully as he plays the instrumental background to her sing-song, which gradually becomes more and more ominous and macabre. Everyone in the bar glares at Dawn as if she had been reduced to a piece of meat, as she notices several of the patrons, both male and female, hold up the peace sign while they flick their forked tongues in between their two fingers. Dawn wakes up and realizes it had been another bad dream.

Dawn slips into a hysterical crying spell, spontaneously falling apart over misplaced earrings. These were earrings that Cheri had once given her that she had accidentally lost since.

"Why are you crying over this?" Cheri asked, confused. "I'm not mad. They're just earrings."

"You're not making me feel any better," Dawn said. Dawn was quickly losing her taste for life, as it was progressively losing its flavor. Her new trait of hypersensitivity was merely indicative of her fragmentation.

Since Wolf had selflessly lifted and absorbed Joy's curse, sacrificing himself for his faithful companion, Dawn had returned to being her old self...well, not really. Cheri was determined to bring Dawn out of her rut, and replace the joy that Joy had stolen. She took Dawn shopping for some funky new threads to try and cheer her up, and Dawn let her...begrudgingly. As they browsed through the outfits in the overpriced store, Rick Springfield's good time tune, *Where's All the Love*, from his *Wait For Night* album, came on over the intercom.

Cheri spots a woman wearing a long fur coat that looks to be made from Alaskan polar bear. Dawn looks at Cheri, as if asking her to do something. Cheri and Dawn nearly ambush the woman in an alley, until they learn that she owns a ritzy antique shop that sells vintage clothing. Dawn later has her pick at taking whatever she wishes, in exchange for the woman's life. It's here that Cheri finds a Western, fringe vest, which she feels looks more dainty and appropriate for Dawn. She also gets Dawn a Cowboy-type belt and a pair of suede, Western chaps to accompany the upgraded look.

Before permanently departing the wicked land of the United States, Cheri and Dawn decided to treat themselves to one last girls' night on the town. They found a dive bar that was practically within walking distance from the *San Francisco International Airport*.

Cheri thought that maybe a few drinks might help drown Dawn's turmoil a bit, of which she definitely had her lion's share. Dawn had been looking at Cheri in a way that left her to ponder if Dawn was silently asking for help, or plotting to snap Cheri's neck like a twig. Either way, nothing was going to change Cheri's doting adoration for Dawn, not even her distant attitude or eagerness to push her away.

As the two semi-estranged lovers sat side by side on the stools, the wily bartender hit on both of them. They didn't embrace his proposition, but they had grown tired of constantly fighting off suitors, so they did accept some psychedelic mushrooms from him. As they tripped on these, even Dawn began to relax while they watched the devious bartender pretend to not drool over them. He, like every other man, fantasized about slipping them his 'beefy' tube steak, not realizing that he didn't stand a chance in Hell at getting with either of them. This fact, however, did not dissuade the overly confident dum-dum from trying to achieve his underhanded and unsavory goal.

Just as Cheri noticed that the gloom on Dawn's face wasn't fading, a young woman got up on the makeshift stage, which was more of a cardboard platform, and began doing a performance-art piece. Cheri sipped on her Bloody Mary, trying to get her younger, stoned lover to share it with her. She knew that Dawn preferred moonshine, but it was illegal and therefore not sold in legitimate establishments, and Dawn was once again without a proper baby bottle. Granted, this second flask had been cursed and therefore not as missed, but Dawn liked what she liked, and was stubborn when it came to anything unfamiliar. The amateur entertainer had introduced herself to the patrons as, *Karen*, which made Dawn think about the Karen she had gotten to know, who believed to know everything about the Bible, and whom Julie had once called, *Care-Wren*, to illustrate how Karen…not unlike most Christians…wasn't nearly as caring as she appeared to be.

Since Dawn was in her own little world, and didn't seem to know that Cheri was even with her, the pink-haired Cambion decided to step outside for some fresh air. Cheri wanted to say her goodbyes to her Van anyway, which she would soon be abandoning, to take Dawn to Europe. She notices that the car beside them has three toddlers inside, all only a year or two apart, strapped in car seats with the windows rolled up. The owner had left the keys turned, keeping the radio on. Judas Priest's, *Breaking the Law*, is blaring through the speakers and the windows, at a volume that is ridiculously threatening to the children's ear drums. Stepping around to the front of the car, she looks intently at the center of the hood, and uses her mind to disconnect and dismantle the engine. She then goes back into the bar to see if she can sniff out the despicable mother who abandoned her kids outside.

Dawn is still in blank mode, numb and oblivious to where she is or who she's with. Cheri uses her keen intuition and her supernatural hearing to pinpoint the guilty party. She overhears part of a conversation between two women that signal to her that she has found the unfit mother. She quickly interjects herself into the garish discussion. The two women are heavily intoxicated, so they don't mind any. Cheri, on the other hand, minds when they both mispronounce her name.

"It's pronounced, *Cherry*," she corrected the two boozed-up bimbos, noticing that Dawn was still sitting alone several feet away and staring quietly into space.

"So, have you had any luck tonight, Cheri?" one of the women asked her, once again mispronouncing her name with a 'Sh' sound.

"No, have you?" Cheri asked back, playing along and picking her battles.

"This fucking place has gotten boring for us. We've blown every regular here, at least twice. She has, anyway," the woman admitted boastfully and shamelessly, referring to her whorish friend, whom Cheri noticed was wearing a wedding ring.

Cheri excuses herself and waits outside, after sharing some small talk with the two slutty women. The two harlots eventually leave the bar, drunk of their asses, and the one friend leaves the pregnant one to drive herself home. The lousy excuse for a mother doesn't even notice that her car is dead. As she opens the door, Cheri sneaks up behind her and whacks her over the head, knocking the woman to the ground. Cheri stands over her, holding up the rock as if intending to stone her again.

"Please," the woman begs. "I'm pregnant!"

Cheri looks in the windows at the children, who are frightened but not vocal about it. "Trust me, bitch. I'm doing your baby a favor. At least the kid inside of you will go to Heaven this way, not having you as a mother."

With that, Cheri brings the rock down, striking her right between the eyes, killing her and her unborn child. After Cheri stones the heartless adulterer, she is attacked by a group of men.

"Hey dyke," one of the cocky assholes said, chuckling. "Come here, dyke. Come here. Come on. Come to Papa," he said, patronizing her and treating her like a dog.

His buddies just laughed and cheered him on, psyched to see some hot action. They were so caught up in their ignorant hatred, that they didn't even notice that Cheri had just murdered someone. They had noticed her eyeballing the two women in the pub, and assumed that she was lusting after them. These were upstanding men who were active in the local Christian community, who were immense bigots against anyone who was different. The desensitized kids in the car continued to remain silent, as they calmly watched what was going on outside.

"Ooohhh boy," Cheri said, "have you guys picked the wrong woman at the wrong time."

Dawn had been observing the changes between the setting of the 70s and the rising of the 80s, and didn't like what she was seeing. People were putting down the bongs and joints, smoking arsenic and cyanide instead. Marijuana had completely been forgotten and outdated, replaced by lines of cocaine, which made people violent and paranoid instead of enlightened and free. Men had begun wearing Hawaiian shirts, who weren't at all ethnic. *Gay* no longer meant *happy*, but *queer*. Afros had been replaced with hair that looked like it had been struck by lightning.

She had seen a man who looked like a cross between a peacock and a rooster, with his multi-colored, 3ft mohawk. The women wore skimpy bikinis in public, who were too often those who had no business wearing such revealing clothing. Men had exchanged their disco shirts for *Members Only* jackets. New trends had taken over, where teenagers were stretching their ears and gauging their lobes to the extreme where they looked alien and inhuman.

Pinball machines and *Polaroid* memories had replaced the pleasures of nature and the experiences of life. She saw houses and bars decorated with Christmas tree lights around the windows and doors, when it was nowhere near *tis the season*. Dawn spotted parents walking their kids on leashes, which both disturbed her and reminded her of how much she misses her dead son. Dance clubs began to disappear, as Americans traded the word *boogie* for *aerobicize*. Americans were more upset over the gas shortages than they were about the *Three Mile Island* meltdown that they had already forgotten entirely.

Children still ate *Pop Rocks* and read comic books. The Cold War was still raging. There was still the occasional streaker, and families still ate fondue. However, Dawn could see that more Americans were becoming materialistic and consumer-motivated, while less were continuing to be laid back, open minded, and experimental. Those that remained free spirits were quickly persecuted, punished, and prosecuted by the system. More men began using curlers than women, and the fragrance of the almighty dollar became more important than how people's hair smelled.

The radical and countercultural Movements dissipated as if they had never existed, replaced with self-absorption and shallow obsessions. Corporate America was on the rise more than ever before, and the land of the free and home of the brave was on a fast track to greed and apathy. The hippie had withered away, and the yuppie was born. The country was changing, and Dawn…in her intuitive wisdom…did not like what she was seeing, insightful and enlightened enough to know that it would only get worse from here. The pep of her era had been replaced with cynicism and callousness.

Dawn had grown weary of taking advantage of people just to barely survive. She had exhausted her devious tactics and deeds of retribution. She was tired, burnt out, and just wanted it all to be over. She had dedicated such time and energy toward laying the groundwork for vengeance, that she could no longer stand to see her own reflection in the mirror anymore. Her hatred for mankind had involuntarily empowered the *Labynkyr Devil* and turned her into what she despised the most. She had become a monster, who was now no different and no better than Nurse Carl.

Dawn would catch herself in a trance, playing with green *Clackers* just to pass the time and kill the tedious, mundane days that had plagued and haunted her. She adored Cheri, but the only excitement she had left to look forward to was when they would make love. So, although their relationship was not based on sex, the lovemaking had become the only moments when Dawn would smile. Having said that, Dawn wasn't nearly as happy as she led Cheri to believe, which was why the sex between them had become nonexistent.

Dawn meditated and reflected on her life for the first time since Reuben was taken from her arms. She realized that sex didn't thrill her anymore, as if the fire had been extinguished. She loved being with Cheri and enjoyed doing what she could to please her, but deep down, sex had just lost its magic. It just didn't get her wet and bothered anymore. The only thing that aroused her that way now, was blood. She preferred to trick herself into believing that most of the people she had killed were bad seeds, detestable and nefarious characters, but she had reached the point where she just didn't care either way. God was no respecter of persons and neither was she, at least not anymore. Her insatiable lust for bloodshed was no longer discriminate. Dawn realized that she had become the monster that she despised in others, and it terrified her. She was helplessly moonstruck over murder, regardless of the rhyme or reason.

People from both genders gave Dawn lecherous stares as she and Cheri moved through the San Francisco airport. Cheri had put Dawn's hair up in a French twist, trying to get her psyched for the anticipated escapade. Dawn, however, was sadly unreceptive to Cheri's efforts.

"So, do you think we'll get laid when we get off the plane?" Cheri asked, subtly hinting to Dawn that she hoped for them to get frisky in the most romantic city on the planet.

"I think you're thinking of Hawaii," Dawn said, not getting Cheri's intended meaning.

Seeing Dawn's lingering lack of enthusiasm, it broke her heart to figure that her Cherokee lover had died. Dawn still had breath in her lungs, but no life in her spirit. It was like walking with a zombie, as they made their way to their assigned Gate. As they quietly sat next to each other, waiting to board their plane, Cheri tried to maintain the facade of strength, as Dawn held her droopy face in her hands. People around them noticed Dawn's melancholy, wondering how someone so pretty, who was flying to somewhere so enchanting, could be so down and depressed. Little did they know that Dawn had become a stranger to Cheri more than they could ever be. One man boldly approached the two ladies, observing the tension between them, and held out his hand to Cheri.

"Would you like a little something to make life seem a little sweeter?" he asked, as he presented a handful of mixed pills to the raspberry queen.

Cheri just glanced up at him, giving him the evil eye, using her body language to make it clear that it was in his best interest to walk away.

"Menage a twat," he said softly but angrily under his breath, as he turned and walked clear across to the other side of the transit lounge, even though he had previously been sitting only feet away from the pair of smashing beauties.

About an hour later, Dawn is still sitting next to Cheri in the terminal, waiting for their delayed flight. Dawn is wearing a scarf over her face, covering everything but her eyes. Her hair had also been cut short, at her request, and this time…it didn't grow back right away. She was ashamed of where she had been and what she had done, desperately feeling the urgent need to hide and conceal herself from others. Everything Dawn had done had been for survival or resulted from the reprehensible maltreatment she received from others. She was a product of her environment and an outcast of society, and yet she couldn't see how sublime she was. Cheri sat cross-legged, reading a copy of *Teen Beat*, while Dawn noticed some college jocks staring and snickering in her direction.

"Hey, Alex…Check out the chica over there," one of them said, proving his ignorance by insolently mistaking Dawn's olive complexion for a Mexican.

"Yeah…the muchacha doesn't appear to have any proper respect for the fucking animal kingdom," the equally and brazenly bigoted, Alex, said back.

Dawn was wearing a suede jacket that had a fancy fur collar. It was something Cheri had acquired for her, thinking that it would make her feel like Wolf was still with her. Dawn's naysayers were the definition of hypocrisy, as her accuser's girlfriend was sitting there on his lap, holding an authentic alligator purse that bore an actual head of a baby alligator on the front flap.

Dawn remained calm and meek. There was a time when she would have risked the consequences from ripping these frat boys to shreds. But, that time had passed, along with her days of gyrating against Cheri's pink parts. She had regained her strength, but not so much her will. She just didn't care enough to bother anymore, as life had robbed her of something precious that she could never retrieve.

Besides, she knew who she was, especially when it came to her love for animals. It didn't matter what anyone else said or thought. Alex Pacheco founded the *PETA* organization earlier that year, in March. *PETA* became a remunerative organization that is known for it's fondness for animals and contempt for humans. In this way, they became the antithesis of the Christian church, who make it a point to praise humans and piss on animals. In a perfect world, we would have a third option that fell somewhere in the middle.

OCTOBER 27, 1980
BLUE MOON
PARIS AIRPORT

Before leaving California, they drove past the *Black House*, on California St, where Zeena LaVey and her celebrity father held the *Church of Satan*. They then drove over five hours, from San Francisco to Chatsworth (just outside Los Angeles), to visit *Santa Susana Pass Road*. They parked Cheri's van on *Iverson Road* and hiked to the 500-acre location of the *Spahn Movie Ranch* (where Charles Manson and his *Family* had communally lived). A wildfire had destroyed all the film sets and residential structures, in September of 1970, so there wasn't much left to see. In spite of this, both Cheri and Dawn could still feel the haunting energy that was left behind and still lingered at the infamous property.

The stagnant lovers then departed for the land of love, from *LAX*. The long flight seemed like it would last for decades, but after nearly twelve hours, they reached their final destination. The *Charles De Gaulle* Airport was crowded and disorganized, in complete chaos. Before they were allowed to do anything, they had to be analyzed by customs. As they stood in what appeared to be an eternal line, the man in front of them turned to address them. Like Cheri, he was a white American, but was there with his wife and three stepkids who were all mixed race.

"You two are registered Americans, I assume?" he asked, boldly.

"Yeah," Cheri answered unenthusiastically, while Dawn hung her head and stayed out of it, keeping to herself.

"Well, I feel led to warn you. When you get up there, they're going to ask you why you're here in their country. Regardless of what your real reason is, it's always best to tell them you are here for pleasure and to see the sights. Otherwise, they'll give you the third degree, put you in a holding room, confiscate your passports, and threaten to detain you indefinitely. I've seen it too many times."

"Wow, thank you for the heads up," Cheri said in gratitude, while secretly not worried about it. She knew, if anyone gave them any trouble, she could use her powers of mind control to remedy the problem.

It felt like a millennium to get through the line, but as soon as they did, they moved smoothly through the gate with no dispute or harassment. Many of the visitors and tourists go straight to the restaurants and boutiques, while Cheri feels pressed to answer a call from nature. While the raspberry hybrid is using the Parisian restroom, the waiting Dawn is approached by a cluster of vampire enthusiasts who are obsessed over the conspiracy that they exist. They try to sell her one of their vampire kits, which is a coffin-shaped wooden briefcase that holds a wooden stake, 2 silver bullets, a small vial of holy water, and a single garlic clove. This makes Dawn think about Reuben, and how unbearably miserable she had continued to be without him, not to mention the wrenching agony that came with losing their only son.

"I'm not interested," she told the vampire worshippers, putting her hand up to further show them that she wouldn't take their bait.

As the gothic zombies wandered off to sell their vampire pitch to the next gullible chump, Dawn quickly brushed her eyes with her hands, trying to wipe her tears away and keep them from coming out. Cheri came walking out of the ladies' room looking just as vulnerable as the vampire posers had hoped Dawn would be.

"What's wrong?" Dawn asked. "Did something happen in there?"

"It's not a ladies' room," Cheri educated.

"You walked into the wrong one?" Dawn inquired, assuming her friend hadn't been paying attention and mistakenly entered the men's room instead.

"No," Cheri said, with a facial expression that looked as uncomfortable as Dawn now was around her, or anyone for that matter. "The restroom is co-ed.

Something tells me that all of the toilettes are going to be co-ed here."

As they moved through the Parisian airport, they both noticed that all the eateries were only open at certain hours of the day. The French only ate at designated times, unlike so many fat Americans who nibbled and munched 24/7. Though this difference came as another eye-opener for them, it wouldn't be the last surprise. Dawn didn't have an appetite anyway, other than for blood and moonshine. Cheri didn't feel like dining either, since she could feel Dawn slipping away again. As the two estranged lovebirds walked out and exited the airport, little did they know that they were being watched. As luck would have it, a taxi just happened to be pulling in front of the doors as they came out.

"Vous dames besoin d'un ascenseur?" he asked them, through the rolled down, front passenger window. The side of the taxi had a logo on the doors, of a spear laying underneath a shield with a snake design.

"We don't speak French," Cheri told him.

"You dames need a lift?" he repeated semi-rudely, this time so they could understand.

Cheri looked over at Dawn, who stood beside her but was still somewhere else in her head. "That'd be great," Cheri answered, now looking back at the cabbie.

"So, what brings you to France? Where you ladies headed?" he inquired, as Cheri helped Dawn into the back seat and then climbed in herself. "Is your young friend okay?" he asked, observing that the silent Dawn looked dead inside.

"She's fine," Cheri answered, in denial. "Do you know of any decent apartments around here, preferably ones that aren't insanely overpriced?" she asked him, while Dawn quietly stared out her window.

"I actually might know a good place," he replied.

Cheri peeked at his dashboard and saw his ID badge, reading the name, *Cerneus Herne*. Dawn stared at the motos that were parked on the sidewalk and the scooters that were delivering food.

"You dames got lucky."

"How so?" Cheri questioned.

"Most of the taxi drivers here are *malhonnete*, meaning they're dishonest. If they detect you're a tourist, they'll take you for a much longer ride than necessary or flat out mug you."

"I see," Cheri said, in a pessimistic tone. "You're different, I take it?"

"I have no interest in taking advantage of you and your friend," he reassured. "Like I said, you dames got lucky."

They finally pulled up in front of what appeared to be a reasonable-looking apartment complex.

"How much do I owe you?" Cheri asked.

"Do you have any euros?" he asked her.

Cheri suddenly realized that they hadn't thought to check to see where to exchange their currency, while they were still at the CDG airport. The whole concept had never even crossed their mind. Cheri felt really stupid and embarrassed, not sure how to get them out of this predicament.

"Don't worry about it," he told her. "It's my treat."

"I'm so sorry," Cheri apologized. "Are you sure? Thank you, sir," she expressed her gratitude again, while Dawn lifted their luggage out of the small trunk.

"No worries, mam. Just remember to trade your currency for euros. Not everyone here will be as forgiving as me."

"I understand," Cheri said.

Cheri thanked him once more for being so unexpectedly kind, returning his friendly wave as he watched them both go inside the building. Dawn carried their bags, which she didn't mind doing, especially since her superhuman strength had returned. At that moment, Cerneus's ears dropped off the sides of his head and were replaced with deer ears. Antlers sprouted just above where the human ears had shed. His hair was still long and curly. He wore a Celtic torc around his neck, which was basically a heavy ring of jewelry that resembled a coiled snake.

NOVEMBER 6, 1980
MAD MOON

Dawn and Cheri had already moved, now shacking up in an extravagant apartment, where they had flocked to after inconspicuously disposing of the former residents. Dawn still struggled to deal with the post-traumatic stress from losing Wolf. Cheri could see the intense pain in her trophy girlfriend's eyes. They were in the most romantic destination on the planet and currently had free room and board in the upgraded space, but it apparently wasn't enough.

The only pleasure that Dawn found was in an *Ocarina* whistle, which Cheri had gotten for her when Dawn got her vest. Dawn played the flute beautifully, enjoying the indigenous sound it made, which reminded her of her Native heritage.

"What if someone comes knocking for the two women we just killed?" Dawn asked, referring to the two sisters who had just recently bought the apartment they had been renting for years.

"Don't worry, baby," Cheri told her. "If I need to, I can mess with people's minds, so that they think they see someone else when they look at us."

As the dormant lovers chatted, Dawn sat on the toilet, which had been installed in this tiny closet that had zero walking space. There was no mirror and no sink, just a toilet and a bidet beside it. Cheri stood outside the narrow stall, talking to her while she did her business. Cheri reached into her jacket pocket and pulled out a flyer that someone had handed her at the airport, which she had folded up and forgotten about. Paris was hosting their first ever Furry Convention. The more Cheri stared at this promotion, the more excited she became. This advertisement looked to be beyond the call of the wild, as it was clearly a taboo event where inhibitions would be left at the door. She knew how much Dawn loved animals, and foolishly thought that something like a fetish event might help bandage her scars. Though Cheri wasn't fond of the idea of sharing Dawn with others, she was desperately willing, at this point, to do whatever it took to bring Dawn back to life.

This anticipated Con was within walking distance from their new home, so Cheri thought it'd be nice to take a relaxing stroll. As they did this, it didn't take long for Dawn and Cheri to notice another difference between the US and France. There was dog shit all over the sidewalks. Not only was it obvious that dogs were widely beloved, but it became clear that there were no laws to enforce French citizens to pick up after their pets. They also quickly found out that France had a lot of dirt and cobblestones, and the people did a ton of walking.

There were cars, but they appeared to be all the same. The cars were much smaller, more compact, and seemed to be of the same make. This was due to the French preferring to support French-made brands. It was also evident that cars were permitted to park wherever they pleased. Not only were the cars parked on sidewalks, but the motorbikes seemed to have free reign as well.

All the men whistled at Dawn and Cheri both, checking out their butts as they passed by. They were used to this attention, so it didn't shock them. The only difference was that all of their French admirers appeared to be heavy smokers. Before getting to the Convention, they came upon an outdoor staircase that was monumental in its number of steps.

"What the fuck!" Cheri complained, as they both glanced up at what appeared to be an endless amount of steps. "There must be at least three hundred steps here," she guessed.

"Come on," Dawn invited. "Get on my back."

"You have to be kidding," Cheri said. "You can't carry me up this ridiculous mountain."

"Yes, I can. Trust me."

"I can't ask you to do that, honey. This stairway is enormous. I'd be too afraid that you'd hurt your back. I'll be fine. It's okay," Cheri politely declined, not willing to risk her health, even though she wasn't exactly happy about Dawn's cold shoulder.

Dawn appreciated Cheri's genuine concern for her, but was also confident in what she was capable of. Before Cheri could put up a fight, Dawn had turned her back, knelt down, grabbed Cheri's legs, and lifted her friend up onto her back. Then, with the helpful combination of adrenaline and determination, she effortlessly scaled those steps while overwhelmingly impressing the older, and somewhat heavier, Cheri. Dawn may have turned frigid in certain ways, but she still had a fringe benefit or two to offer.

This was an invitation-only weekend where attendees came dressed as their favorite animals. The adult Convention was being held at a lavish four-star hotel, which had basically been rented out for the erotic occasion. The costumes were obnoxiously cartoony, as if they had been snatched from the theme park storage room. The difference was that these costumes were modified to be equipped with a buttoned flap that covered both the backside and the crotch region. This was no nerd celebration, but rather a social gathering for disguised perverts to meet, mingle, and mate. Dawn and Cheri had come unprepared, only having their regular clothes on their backs.

"It's okay, sweetheart," Cheri said, unwilling to stand by and watch her girlfriend become comatose again. "I can fix this."

Cheri took her precious Dawn into the restroom, where it was once again co-ed, and waited until it was empty. Cheri squinted her eyes, focusing on herself and Dawn. Within a matter of seconds, they were both endowed with appropriate costumes. Dawn was now dressed as a brown wolf and Cheri as a red fox, even though they were basically at a cathouse. Their costumes, of course, weren't real, but to the rest of the patrons, they were. Cheri had been able to create the illusion that they were dressed as animals, when in reality, nothing had changed.

Dawn and Cheri didn't have sex with anyone, but did let the interested parties sniff and lick their butts. They used their innate charm to seductively trick men and women into buying them drinks, under the luring guise of false promises. They were even able to discreetly coerce one gentleman, who had boasted about how wealthy he was, to sign over everything he had to them. Dawn wasn't proud of this decision, but knew they didn't have a choice. Neither one of them were hirable or fluent, so they weren't really in any position to turn down money.

Watching the others get it on in the open, got them hot and bothered, and made for spectacularly euphoric sex for when they returned to their flat. Cheri's plan had worked and Dawn had opened up to her again, at least temporarily. This time, being with Cheri didn't drain her life energy like before. Either Dawn had grown immune to Cheri's vampiric power, or Cheri had somehow turned it off.

Meanwhile, Agent Shelling is trying to deal with the aftermath of what he has become. The fact that he had evolved to be the very thing he hated most, had finally hit him and was now making him sick. Not only had he failed William, by not finding and no longer caring to catch his killer, but he had become a killer himself. Shelling had noticed that the 70s were over too, as well as his career with the federal government. He knew how important God was to his late nephew and had tried to honor that. This, however, progressively became more difficult, the longer that Dawn got away with everything. He just didn't give a shit anymore, no matter how much he had loved his family or how hard he had tried to avenge them.

As he drives his car through the blackness of night, he remembers a sermon that he had heard years back…a story about Cain. After God had banished him, casting him out of Eden for murdering his brother, the Gospel says that Cain was not only struck with an identifying mark, but was stricken with paralyzing fear of being hunted and killed by a mysterious enemy that the Scriptures never clarify, specify, or elaborate on. Some Christians (those few who are more open-minded and less know-it-all) speculate that this may have been Biblical evidence to support the existence of extraterrestrial life. Shelling would have shrugged this thought off when he was younger, when he was more of a skeptic, but Dawn had changed all that. He knew that Dawn was a werewolf, and if werewolves existed, then why not aliens?

Agent Shelling had been in Texas for months and had gotten nowhere with his tireless search for Dawn. It was incomprehensible, inconceivable, and unacceptable that this unusual suspect had eluded him for what seemed to be indefinite in her impressive and infinite evasion. His once-flourishing career had earned him the stellar reputation of being a champion in his field. He was accustomed to triumph, not defeat, and his pathetic failure at tracking and hunting Dawn was not sitting well with his inflated ego. This inability to catch her had caused him to question if he had lost his aptitude, or if he had simply never had it to begin with.

The Bureau had informed him that they had become indifferent and were even considering granting Dawn clemency. They had lost faith that she would ever be captured and had decided that they didn't care either way anymore. Agent Shelling had refused to forfeit or compromise his quest for justice, and had long remained undaunted, though he found himself alone in his ideals. He was willing to sacrifice, even if it jeopardized his own safety or occupational security. The corroborating evidence on Dawn Moon was too substantial, and even if it hadn't been, he needed someone…anyone…to blame and punish. This was a personal war for him, and he was in it for the sweet taste of victory. However, that was then, and this was now. He just didn't care anymore, and had become hard-bitten like everyone else.

Based on the hair samples and DNA evidence that he had analyzed and collected since his search for her first launched, he had a blacksmith make him customized ammunition that was made of mercury. Though his apathetic superiors thought him to be damaged goods, he was convinced that Dawn Moon was a werewolf. As if this wasn't enough to make him appear to be batshit crazy, Dawn had crept into his head and gotten under more than just his skin. The deteriorating federal agent was, in a sense, falling for her. His murderous obsession had bled, and blended, into a deranged passion. This warped mindfuck made him question his morality and doubt his conscience. His lustful desire for her made him hate himself, which only drove him further over the edge and motivated his death wish for her.

Aside from these quicksilver bullets, he had gone through the trouble of finding the poisonous plant, *Wolfsbane*, and liquefying it into a syringe. Now that he was no longer searching for her or working for the Bureau, he pondered the idea of using this weaponry on random, innocent animals or school age children.

As he battled these conflicting inner demons of pride and self-loathing, he found his inconsistent thoughts drifting off to another painful subject that he had never fully recovered from or moved passed. His last ex-wife, whom he hadn't seen in years, had burned him in a way that was unforgivable and inhumane. The ungrateful bitch had taken everything from him, including his very soul, after all he did to happily give her his unending devotion and unconditional love. Not only had she used their sham marriage as a ploy for embezzling tactics and sadistic schemes, but she turned out to be a blissful prostitute and deadly sociopath. His nephew had not been the only one who had been brutally murdered by an unhinged serial killer.

His sinister ex-wife had butchered him, just not physically. What was most insulting and embarrassing about what Susan proved to be, was that she was a baptized Christian, or at least allegedly and superficially. She had been no more committed to God than she had been to him. She was a pseudo-Christian, and merely one of the infinite number he had regretfully encountered and trusted in his lifetime. He wasn't perfect either, nor had he ever professed to be, but he knew the difference between flawed and fraud.

Shelling's eyes burned with his own tears, as his hands began to violently shake again, feeling another panic attack coming on. His vision blurred and his chest felt like an elephant was sitting on it. He couldn't breathe or concentrate. Susan had taken something from him that he could never get back, and the dull knife she had left in his back only twisted and deepened as the days passed. Time was not on his side, and apparently neither was God. He had learned the hard way, once too many, that God doesn't answer prayers, but instead was the original Indian giver. He had also learned that people don't come back or give second chances. God never protected him from being hurt, or punished the wicked who rejoiced in damaging others.

It tormented him to picture Susan looking into someone else's eyes and telling another man what she swore was reserved for him alone, but he knew that she would never genuinely love anyone but herself. As much as it killed him to imagine her giving herself to another man, he finally began to accept, as painful and difficult as it was, that she had been a stranger for the five years she pretended to be his, and that the meanings of *commitment* and *love* were alien to her. She had redefined the term, *alienation*, for him, and completely destroyed his opinion of marriage.

The discouraged and demolished federal agent drove recklessly down the road, after visiting the local liquor store. He had completely lost his way and entirely drifted from Dawn's addictive scent. He had steered so far off course, that he doubted whether or not he could get back on. It got dark and his poor night vision had taken effect, so he squinted and strained to see the patch of road in front of him that was illuminated by his headlights.

Agent Shelling had just learned that his brutal ex-wife had gotten married to one of the many male adulterers she had proudly betrayed him with, and though he hated to admit it, it still stung…he still loved her…and the fact that he still cared for her the way he did, tormented him, because he knew she would never want him back or give him a second thought. He had been emasculated, and had become a reluctant yet advocate misogynist. As he put more miles on his car, he generously sipped on the bottle of *Southern Comfort*, which he held warmly between his legs.

As the night hours got later and the sky got darker, the road got emptier. Agent Shelling had the radio on, listening to a talk show where they were discussing Admiral Richard E. Byrd's alleged encounter with an extraterrestrial race of Nazis, in a secret city somewhere in Antarctica, during 1947. He began to feel his eyelids get heavy, as he caught himself struggling and forcing to hold them open. He knew that he should pull over and rest, but his determination and bitterness fueled his energy to keep moving. His neck became really stiff, and his lower back got so sore that he shuffled and shifted in his seat to try and temporarily relieve some of the pressure and discomfort.

He noticed that his steering wheel began to feel as if it was turning on its own. While this happened, the front windshield froze up and frosted over, which was illogical and impossible since the hot air was on full blast. Just to be sure, he placed his hand over the air vents to check the working condition of the blower, and sure enough, the heater core was operating perfectly. Yet, somehow the cabin of the vehicle had become unbearably chilled. Agent Shelling used the wipers to try and defrost the ice that had caked on his windshield, but the more he fought it, the harder it got.

Shelling heard a deafening hiss come from nowhere, which quickly brushed over the roof of his issued, 1975 *Chrysler* Newport. His baby-blue car briefly glowed with magnificent radiance, as it rattled and shook from side to side, while involuntarily reacting to the saucer that had buzzed above. As this otherworldly sound passed over him, he saw a blinding white ball move ahead and then abruptly shift to the right, inevitably crashing into the field that waited off the side of the road. The disgruntled and disturbed Agent immediately panicked, instinctively trying to pull over. The obnoxious light blinded him from being able to see and something resisted when he slammed on the breaks, which refused to let him stop.

The car was now driving itself. He could see his own breath, which was like fog coming from his mouth. His eyes widened in fear and disbelief, as he looked at the center of his front windshield and saw the painful image of his ex-wife's face there in icy mist. Before he could fully process what he was experiencing, the car stopped all on its own. No one else was on the road, so he was the only eye witness to this unanticipated and unbelievable phenomenon, which had tragically come at the wrong time to the worst man.

Cautiously stepping out of the car, he found himself in an open field. Though it was nearly 3am, he was in the middle of a bright and blinding circle. Above him, in the night sky, was something that could only be compared to the *Northern Lights*. It was beautiful but unusual. About thirteen feet in front of him, was a mass that was ovoid and opaque. He could see specks and sections that looked to be comprised of flashy chrome, but the white light concealed and overpowered much of the monopolizing detail. As Agent Shelling nervously walked closer to the light, he felt a strange warmth in the otherwise cold, Nebraska air. There were no flames, explosion, or combustion, and no threatening hint of peril in sight. As he moved in to inspect closer, the white light began to diminish and expose what appeared to be a strange craft of some sort. Though he couldn't see any visible damage, he conjectured that the unidentified object had crash landed. The oval-fashioned spaceship appeared to be made out of a shiny metal, but one unlike he had ever seen. The foreign aircraft had a swastika embedded on the face of it. He couldn't find any evidence of a door or window.

The FBI agent noticed a body that had clearly been catapulted from the craft, on impact. It resembled the figure of a human female, but with lime green complexion. She was completely nude, and looked, by human calculations, to be somewhere in her mid-twenties. As Agent Shelling fearlessly moved closer to her, he noticed that her body was the only part of her that looked homo sapien. She had an abnormally high forehead, while her eyes were freakishly large and solid black. The rest of her facial features and the shape of the lower half of her head were normal, aerodynamic, and oddly alluring. Most men would have turned and ran, but then again, Agent Shelling had proven repeatedly that he wasn't most men.

He suddenly felt an insatiable anger brush over him, much in the same way that the strange light had swept over his vehicle. As he inspected the injured female extraterrestrial, all he could think about was Susan and how she had boastfully wounded and callously abandoned him. Even the way the slender, yet buxom, alien was lying in the grass, turned him on. She was resting on her side, and the firm, shapely curve of her backside immediately captured his attention. Before either one of them knew it, he had kicked his pants off and mounted her forcefully from behind.

His phallic mojo was rising especially stiff that night, which was delightfully unexpected, as he normally dealt with erectile dysfunction. He mercilessly sodomized the green girl. She tried to fight him off, but was too weak from the traumatic crash. He reached around and covered her mouth with one of his hands. Shoving his middle finger in her lips, he demanded that she suck it with enthusiasm, as he aggressively raped her up the butt. As he violated her ass, his mind wrestled with mixed feelings of love and hate towards Susan.

A couple of cars passed without stopping, but since Agent Shelling and the alien were where they were, all the drivers saw was the blinding light...not them or the ship. Usually, motorists would immediately slow down to get a good look at the carnage. Most people (particularly Christians) love a train wreck, as long as they're not among the victims affected.

After 30 minutes of solid stamina, he threw his head back and howled as if demonically possessed, while he reached blissful climax and joyfully exploded inside her tight, foreign anus. When Agent Shelling was done with her, he left her there in the country field and even bothered to pick up a stone from the ground to hurl at her. Then, in a confused state of numbness and shock, he slowly made his way back to his ugly, blue *Chrysler*, got in, and continued driving deeper into Nebraska, as if nothing had happened.

"Fucking aliens," he said, as if seeing such a thing was normal. "Why are they green, anyway? Makes no fucking sense. Their planet is red, for God's sake," he said aloud to himself, presuming that any and all extraterrestrials must be from Mars.

NOVEMBER 7, 1980
DARK MOON

The next morning, the injured and defiled alien, along with her seemingly unharmed craft, had vanished with the daylight. Agent Shelling woke up with a debilitating migraine and an all-around achiness. His entire body was sore and feverish. Crawling out of bed, he stumbled into the motel bathroom, like a zombie, and reached for the bottle of *Tylenol*. Picking it up by the lid, the bottle dropped out from underneath, landing on the floor and spilling the pharmaceuticals. The weakened ex-Federal employee, with one hand gripping his lower back, gradually got on his hands and knees to pick up the scattered pills.

His tears hit the linoleum floor like raindrops, as he found himself remembering when Susan would refuse to secure the lids on containers. As the naked Bureaucrat stood back up, he felt an itchy feeling on his balls. He reached down to scratch the underside of his scrotum, only to end up screaming in indescribable pain. Looking down at his shrunken penis, he saw little, green, round-shaped sores and warts spread all over his junk. It didn't take him long to assume that he had contracted some sort of astro-venereal disease.

"Of course," he said aloud to himself, in a sigh of cynical pessimism, just before coughing up a pool of green blood into the bathroom sink. "It would be something like this."

He screamed again with incomparable agony, as he continued to barf up ivy-colored slime. This went on for three hours, until he finally choked on his own space-infected blood, dying there on the filthy floor of the cheap motel.

Dawn and Cheri were out taking a walk, once again having to maze around all the dog poop. It was after nightfall, so the excrement was harder to see for most, but not for them. Then, out of nowhere, a mother and five small children came running up to them.

"Pardon nous, mais l'un ou l'autre d'entre vous a-t-il des changements de rechange?"

"Sorry, but we don't parler any Francais," Cheri informed her.

"Pardon us, but do either of you have any spare change?" she begged, shamelessly and aggressively.

"No, not so much. Sorry," Cheri answered, trying to be polite and respectful about turning them down.

"Please," one of the kids pleaded. "We're hungry."

Cheri found it repugnant that their mother involved her many offspring in her scam. Not only should the woman not have had the kids in the first place, but the fact that she clearly continued to have them, despite the fact that she was incapable of taking care of the ones she already had, was disgusting and unsettling. Cheri and Dawn both felt for the kids, but not at all for their lousy mother. They still continued to walk, now at a faster pace, hoping that the dysfunctional family would take a hint and fall by the wayside.

"If you two can't part with any money, could you maybe sign a petition for world peace?" the mother suggested, showing what kind of physical shape she was in by keeping up with their healthy stride.

"No merci," Cheri said, now turning them down in their own language.

Just then, the allegedly starving mother suddenly pushed Cheri with blunt force. Not only did Cheri topple and stumble to the ground, but she landed face first in a pile of dung.

"No mercy is right," the mother said, laughing along with her equally scheming kids. "Did you have a nice trip? Glad we finally got you both to stop for a second."

Dawn looked at her friend on the ground, and then looked back up at the sniggering family. A man stepped out of the shadows, who had obviously been following them and was part of the con. This guy, unlike the mother and kids, had a knife in his hand. He started to approach Dawn, to further browbeat and dragoon her into complying.

"Maybe you should sign the petition," he insisted, glaring at Dawn, while Cheri was still on her hands and knees, trying to spit out the feces that had gotten in her mouth.

"Okay," Dawn gave in. "Okay. We're sorry. Give me the petition. I'll be proud to sign it," she vowed to obey the pushy, pickpocketing mother.

She handed Dawn the dirty clipboard, with a grin on her face, pleased with herself that she was going to get another signature to use later for all sorts of sabotage and fraud. As soon as she held out the clipboard for Dawn to take, the Cherokee grabbed hold of the woman's wrist, while punching her directly in the face with her free hand. Her male accomplice lunges at Dawn with his blade, just before she snatches the clipboard and strikes him across the face with it. Dawn had hit both of them with such force that her fist went right through the lady's skull, and made the man's head spin around like Linda Blair in, *The Exorcist*.

"I think I'm stronger than I was before," Dawn said quietly to herself, realizing that she didn't simply get her strength back, but that it had doubled, if not tripled.

Dawn just stood there, huffing and puffing, while trying to cool down so she could keep herself from wolfing out. The little accessories had all scattered, terrified after witnessing what became of their parents. Cheri didn't want to admit it to herself, but she was scared to death of Dawn. As much as Cheri still adored her, she wasn't blind to the fact that Dawn had changed.

"What should we do with the bodies?" Cheri asked her. "This isn't exactly the fresh start I had in mind for us," she said, hypocritically.

"Leave them there with the rest of the dog shit," Dawn replied.

DECEMBER 7, 1980
LICHE MOON

Dawn had run away from Cheri, only to find herself in a hole of pitch darkness. It felt like a pit because she was surrounded by what appeared to be a dome of sorts. This seemed to be underground, having no light sourcing from anywhere other than the menacing demon that stood before her. The creature had the physical form of a woman but was clearly not human. She held a scythe in her left hand, and had piercing eyes that were literally flames. Dawn wanted to ask her what her name was, but was too petrified with fear to bring herself to speak.

"I am Lich," she told her. "I have been sent here to show you how to achieve immortality."

As Lich spoke, Dawn noticed that there were no teeth in her mouth, but only filthy cobwebs in the horrifying, dark void. The demon's greasy hair suddenly, and literally, turned into snakes. To be more specific, these were coral snakes, which had red, yellow, and black bands on their slimy scales. These snakes were telling Dawn to end her life, in the same way that Satan had once encouraged Eve to betray Adam.

"You're telling me that you want to make me immortal, but your slithering hair is telling me to take my own life? Which is it?" Dawn asked, uncertain which door this hideous demon was pushing her towards.

Dawn stood there, buck naked, facing this hellish beast, while she felt a cold chill overwhelm her exposed body. Her eyes go funny and now see this snake woman with three heads. Lich suddenly resembles more of a prophetic dragon than a mythological being.

"By killing yourself, you become immortal," she clarified to Dawn, as her voice became more and more of a hissing sound. "The wages of sin is death, but the wage of death is eternal life."

Lich's scythe becomes a glowing conductor, sparking with bursts of electricity. Dawn falls back onto the ground beneath her, which is covered in human ash. The scythe is now a hollow staff that is filled with lightning, making Lich an even more intimidating foe to reckon with. The scythe rumbled with sounds of thunder, making Dawn more terrified than she already was.

As Dawn looked at this medusa monster, she noticed that she was looking into a mirror. She also realized that the evil she was seeing was not her own reflection. The snake woman was in the mirror, but it wasn't Dawn. The mirror shakes and shatters, while Dawn nervously covers her face with her trembling hands, protecting her eyes while she remains sitting in human remains. The sharp shards fly outward towards Dawn, not unlike how sparks once flew out of Dawn for Cheri.

Dawn wakes up from her bad dream, perching on top of her raspberry-flavored lover. Her hands are wrapped securely around the trampire's throat, as she is wolfing-out and ready to kill her. Dawn sees that her hands are full of brisk hair and razor-sharp claws. Cheri isn't dead, but she is clearly unconscious. Dawn realizes, from the disconcerting marks on Cheri's throat, that she must have been strangling her in her sleep. Being withdrawn and distant was one thing, but now she had completely lost control of her tempting impulses. Cheri was no longer safe with her, and Dawn couldn't live with herself if she murdered her maraschino Cheri. She missed her days as a dejected and desolate drifter, before Cheri and Wolf had disrupted her unbearable isolation. She was lonely then, watching stones ripple across the water, but at least she had only herself to hurt.

She once stooped to desperate measures to survive, and now straddled one of the two who brought her back to life. Dawn had inexplicable and unearthly abilities that she couldn't explain, and now the thrill of that power had become impossible to resist. Dawn self-reflected, looking at her own life in an unflinching way, as she carefully crawled off of her pink-haired lover. Secrets began to emerge and unfold in her troubled head, as she finally accepted how disturbed she truly was.

Dawn had unwillingly and unintentionally become a liability to the few she had adored. She had suffered enough prescient visions that occurred in the twilight state of her consciousness, as she woke again and again from sleep. The damage done to her mind was indefinite and irreparable, and she couldn't allow it to materialize into something that she would regret forever. Dawn was essentially the personification of a night terror, but inside her werewolf suit was a vulnerable puppy. The only ones to ever see her tender heart were Reuben, Wolf, and Cheri. Reuben was viciously taken away from her, as was their only son. She had tragically lost Wolf.

"I'll be damned if I'm going to lose you too," she whispered aloud to herself, looking at Cheri's red neck.

As rapturous as Dawn's bloodlust was, her amorphous connection with her loved ones was stronger. Meanwhile, as Dawn was seriously contemplating saying her final farewell, her devoted girlfriend was having crazy dreams of her own. Cheri saw Dawn floating adrift, getting further and further away from her loving arms. The Starbuck song, *Moonlight Feels Right*, plays softly and subtly in the background. Cheri missed Dawn's scent, and wished that her sexy bitch had been more trainable.

"Bad dog!" Cheri shouted out at her, as she quietly wept and watched Dawn's innermost feelings be swept away with the tide.

"I can't get to it right now!" Dawn replied, senselessly, too far away to hear Cheri's call. "Been swamped out here all month!"

The music suddenly changes to, *White Bird*, by the band, *It's A Beautiful Day*. As the 1969 hit plays, a white simurgh flies over Cheri, raining down seeds on her head. The bird had the body of a tiny dog and the wings and head of a falcon.

"It's always darkest before Dawn," the bird whispered to Cheri, but loud enough for her to hear, as it fluttered and flapped its wings.

This white bird disappears into thin air afterwards, vanishing as quickly and as mysteriously as it had appeared. Cheri knew that this was likely the calm before the storm, but she kept telling herself that everything was going to be okay. Just then, everything around her went pitch black.

"I should have been born straight," Cheri muttered to herself. "I should have married some lucky silver fox, had his kids, and worshipped at his feet," she said, convincing herself that life would have been so much easier, had she chosen to go the traditional and more conventional route.

Romance, however, was merely one of the sources of her great heartache. She and Dawn had both come to hear music around them, which nobody else could hear. It was as if their lives had been given their own soundtracks, and it made no difference whether they were asleep or awake. This wasn't a case of having a song stuck in their heads, they actually heard the tunes. Hearing voices was often misjudged as psychotic, which was almost always a legitimate experience or spiritual encounter. Hearing music that wasn't there, on the other hand, was an entirely different story. The two lovebirds were clearly on their way to *Crazy Town*, and the music was just a pit stop. The hippies had trusted in something called, *sonic magic*, where they believed that sound could cure the sick, heal the blind, and change the taste of food. Dawn and Cheri never saw any evidence of that being true, but they did seem to be haunted by sound.

Cheri woke up three hours later, drenched in her own sweat, relieved to find her beloved Dawn lying naked beside her in the fetal position. Dawn's back was to her, as the smooth lesbian slid in closer to spoon her. As she put her moist arm around the sexy Cherokee hybrid, she found Dawn's skin to be dry and cold. Cheri resumed her slumber mode, while Dawn opened her eyes and had only been pretending to sleep.

As Cheri fell back into her dream state, Dawn saw a tall, shaggy abomination standing in front of them. It was a white, three-toed creature, with a long neck and a flat face, that looked at Dawn like she was lunch. This beast was different from the others, as it didn't appear to be hazardous or hostile. In any case, the Cherokee beauty had grown numb to just about everything, so the odds of something scaring her, at this point, were practically slim to none.

"You're worried that God will deny you entrance into Paradise because you're a werewolf," it told her in a gruff voice, effectively reading her mind, as she just laid there speechless and motionless. "Don't be. Romans 11:36 says that everything comes from God, and that you have whatever power you have because of God. In other words, you wouldn't be a werewolf if God didn't want you to be. Your curse is not a mistake, but is by God's very design. Embrace your inner child. Embrace the werewolf."

Dawn was enthralled at its calm demeanor, which was unexpected considering its horrifying appearance. People had been alleging, since the dawn of time, that if you die in your dreams, you die for real. However, Dawn was living proof that this wasn't always the case. She had dreamt of her own death, on several occasions, yet she was still here. The Grim Reaper wasn't out to get her. She was the Grim Reaper.

DECEMBER 8, 1980
WINTER MOON

It was the middle of the night, and Dawn was dreaming about the nasty red dwarf again. "Se noyer," was all he said this time, and he said it repeatedly. Fed up with the leer's games, she grabbed the toothsome, Nain, by his pointed head and threw him in the air just high enough to snatch him by his feet. Holding him upside down by his matching, red fur boots, she screamed in his smug face.

"What the fuck are you saying?! I told you, I don't understand your fucking language!"

"Drown yourself," the devilish dwarf translated his own words, wearing a shit-eating grin as his eyes turned solid black and Dawn awoke from her nightmare. "Drown yourself," she heard him say again, after she opened her eyes.

Dawn violently banged the sides of her head, while blinking hard and grinding her teeth. She kept thinking bad thoughts about harming Cheri, thoughts which she so clearly didn't mean or wish to think. Life had become both demeaning and meaningless for Dawn. The world was a cold place, people were cruel, and her detrimental destiny showed no signs of ever changing for the better.

She had outlived her welcome. She would either become a brute or a burden, and neither option fancied her. She had lost Wolf, whom she had been inseparable with. Life had lost its flavor. It was time to go.

"It's a good day to die," Dawn thought to herself, as repugnant drums and flutes play privately in her head.

It was if these musical beats were from a loathsome, 19th Century Calvary Regiment, with the ever-cowardly General Custer as the conductor. She wondered if animals like her could go to Heaven and hoped that it wasn't out of the question. Dawn had heard the so-called *Christian* Church give their take on it, but she knew better than to take anything they had to say seriously.

She leaned over and kissed her pink-haired lover on the forehead, saying goodbye to her while she rested peacefully. The television was playing the national anthem while showing the American flag, before the network signed off for the night. White noise played on the television set, but in Dawn's head, she heard the TV playing the song, *Sad Eyes*, by Robert John. She didn't want to leave Cheri, but there was simply nothing left for her to give. Life had taken away too much from her, as if it had been pushing her to die since the day of her birth. She loved her raspberry-flavored girlfriend, but it just wasn't enough.

Cheri had dosed off, reading a book called *Dianetics: The Modern Science of Mental Health*, which she had bought at the airport gift shop. Dawn had briefly considered brushing the rainbow blinds aside and using the sliding glass door that led to the balcony of their high-rise, but decided that it would be too messy and scarring for Cheri. Just to be safe, she carefully took the phone off the hook, so it wouldn't wake Cheri before she was gone. It was a press-button phone, as opposed to the rotary ones that Dawn had grown up knowing. Dawn quietly slipped on her fringe vest and the imaginary wolf tooth necklace that Julie had given her, and walked out the door, gently shutting it behind her.

Dawn would have recorded herself with a *VHS* camcorder, but she didn't have access to one. So instead, she left a folded note on the nightstand, telling Cheri how she felt about her, but that their love just wasn't enough to kill her pain. Since Cheri had never let them have their picture taken, she left a crayon drawing that she had done of the six of them. The childish sketch included Reuben, herself, Donnie, Wolf, Julie, and Cheri, and they were all holding hands, as if to insinuate that they were a family. She left this, instead of the *Olan Mills* portrait they never had taken, for Cheri to find.

"If you want to see God, just look in the mirror," she heard the voice of Nikolas Schreck again, who seemed to still haunt her mind. "God is the planets and the comets. Every atom in our bodies was once part of a star. God is the universe, and you are God. Reuben is your star-crossed lover, and he will always be with you. You don't need to off yourself to reunite with him. You were born to kill, not die. Don't deny yourself your birthright. Vengeance is yours. Take it!"

Though the voice Dawn heard sounded like Zeena's boyfriend, she knew that it was Lucifer impersonating him, trying to trick her into selling her soul before giving up her life. "Get behind me, Satan," Dawn immediately said in response. "You're barking up the wrong tree, mother fucker. *Don't repay evil for evil. Don't emulate the cruel behavior of this cold world. Let God transform you into a new creature. The Lord's words are pure as silver.* That's 1 Peter 3:9, Psalm 12:6, and Romans 12:2, bitch."

Before long, she found herself gazing at the body of water in front of her. The moon had a red hue to it that night, as if it was a giant disco ball covered in menstrual blood. This moonlight reflected on the French river, as it waited patiently for Dawn's generous donation. She takes a hit of acid, accompanied with *Demerol* pills, to numb her trip. She then stripped off her clothes and laid them on the ground. Walking in a circle, she urinates around the pile. She was scared to die alone, but she wasn't alone. The Christopher Cross song, *Never Be The Same*, plays in her head, as she hopes that this won't be a goodbye, but a 'hello again' to Reuben.

Once the narcotics kick in, Dawn slowly walks into the sanctity and solace of the Parisian river, forever sealing and signifying the completion of her story in the bitter cold water. She knew not what was to come, or if

God would prove to be empathetic enough to permit her to see her loved ones again. She only knew that her heart was too beautiful for this cold world, and life had become too unbearable to go on alone. Though she still had Cheri, she would always be incomplete without her dominant soulmate, their deceased son, and her feral friend.

"Whoever does not love does not know God, because God is love," Dawn softly quoted 1 John 4:8, counting on this Bible verse to redeem her, since she had nothing but smitten love in her broken heart for her departed lover, their stillborn son, Cheri, Julie, and Wolf.

She cherished her memories of Reuben, in spite the unbearable pain she felt without him. She hoped that her undying love would be enough to win the unconditional love of Christ. The church had proven to have a heart of stone, but she counted on Christ being decent.

"You said in Romans 5:8 that you loved me at my darkest. Forgive me, Jesus," she whispered out loud, as tears streamed down her face. "Remember me, as I step into my own grave." Dawn had nobody to perform her last rites, so she just implored God to consider her prayer. "For whomever comes to me in prayer with a sincere heart, honors and glorifies me. Psalm 50:23, 145:18-19, and Proverbs 15:29. Be gracious, Lord, and hear my prayer. Psalm 4:1."

Dawn could hear the psychedelic 1969 tune, *No Time*, by The Guess Who, playing exclusively in her head. Stepping further into the moonlit river, she could see something new in her reflection. She had grown a third eye that was now directly in the middle of her forehead. A middle-aged passerby spotted her, who stopped dead in shock and astonishment. This seasoned survivor had seen the dark side of love, but none of the wicked women in his past had frightened him more than the young Cherokee he was currently laying eyes on.

"Bisclavret," he murmured, only saying this one word. He stood, frozen in both fear and lust, as he watched the stunning Native American prepare to drown herself. "Rougarou," he added, under his breath. Even though Dawn had never experienced full metamorphosis, at least not so others could tell, this man had the gift of second sight and could see straight through her guise.

While imagining herself walking into her watery tomb, she quoted 2 Timothy 1:7 aloud to herself. "For God gave us a spirit not of fear, but of power, love, and self control," she says, to try and deny her thanatophobia. She also thought of Matthew 6:34, which tells us to not worry about tomorrow.

She let go of the build-up of bitterness and resentment that she had been harboring for most of her life, and forced herself to forgive the countless monsters who had taken such joy from hurting her…not excluding God. She thought about the song, *Come Sail Away*, by Styx.

"Jehovah, Atius Tirawa, Yahweh, Unetlanvhi," she prayed, "I may not understand you or your ways, but I ask that you understand mine. I hope you will show me more empathy and compassion in the afterlife, than you've shown me here. I'm sorry for the words I've said and the things I've done, which have wounded or offended you. I pray that you take into consideration what led me to turning out the way I did. The sins of my father and the wickedness of this cold world have infected me," she says, as she baptizes herself by splashing and rinsing her face. "I have heard it preached that agape love is the only love that matters and that all relationships should come second to our love for you. I also know that sometimes you show us your love by allowing us to love and have the love of another (1 John 4:7-11). Sometimes, if we're lucky, your love comes in the form of a relationship with someone special you place in our path. Reuben, Donnie, Julie, and Wolf mean everything to me. Have mercy on Cheri, as well, as it is not her fault that she comes from what she does. Let us all be together in your heavenly Kingdom, and forgive us for what we need forgiven. Please don't throw us away or turn your back on us, the way everyone else has."

She remembered Hebrews 10:22, which says, *come to God with a sincere heart and believe that he will save you. Be free from the chains of your guilty past, as you cleanse your body with pure water*.

The broken, but beautiful, Cherokee noticed a silvery light that shined over the water's surface, as she slowly entered the Parisian river. It was as if the stars were dancing, and sprinkling their magic on the water. The light, however, was not solely sourced by the moon, but by *Freyja*. She recognized the Norse goddess from literature she had read growing up. The fabled soothsayer of superstition had evidently traveled from Norway to see Dawn drown her sorrows.

Dawn's fear was finally replaced with peace, as she imagined being reunited with Reuben, their son, Julie, and her feral friend. Looking at her nakedness, as she slowly made her way into the freezing water, she noticed that her abnormal body hair was gone. This beastly excess that she had been burdened with for the majority of her life, had mysteriously left her physical being. Though the brisk animal hairs had fallen away, she knew what she still was all the same. She gazed up at the brightly lit *Eiffel Tower*, which she interpreted as the world giving her the middle finger one last time.

"My God, I am ashamed and humiliated. Please forgive me, Jesus! My iniquities have risen higher than my head, and my guilt has reached the heights of Heaven! Let me find you, as I seek you wholeheartedly. Let my mind transform me into what you want me to be. I put on my new self with the love I have in me." Dawn prays loudly, but humbly, desperate for mercy and empathy (Ezra 9:5-6, Jeremiah 29:13, Romans 12:2, Ephesians 4:24, and Colossians 3:10,14).

The pale horse that she had been raised to believe in, never showed up to carry her to Paradise. Dawn's clothes turn to stone from the apotropaic qualities of her piss. As the troubled squaw slowly sinks into the icy Abyss, the tune in her head changes to the Head East song, *Never Been Any Reason.* The chorus, 'Save my life, I'm going down for the last time,' plays in Dawn's unraveled mind, as she has second thoughts a minute too late and tries to swim back up before completely running out of air.

She still has a death wish, but she is suddenly more terrified of what death may bring than she is of living without her loved ones. It's at that moment when a sinister mermaid appears out of nowhere, with a wide mouth of piranha teeth and the strength of a shark. She had three heads and six arms. She used two hands to cover Dawn's mouth and nose, two to dig her claws into her sides, and two to pull her down. This was one of the monsters that Cain had feared, when he was banished from Eden.

Dawn could feel the mercury poisoning leak out from *Eurynome's* hooks and contaminate her bloodstream. She tussled tooth and nail for her empty life, but her struggle was weakened by the silvery mermaid. Dawn's lungs filled up with water, as her eyes closed for the final time. As soon as Dawn was beyond any hope of recovery or resurrection, *Eurynome* turned into wood while still restraining Dawn's fresh corpse. The silver mermaid did this so that the corpse-eating goddess, *Cerridwen*, wouldn't be able to take her beautiful prize for herself. Dawn was too precious a treasure to let slip.

The three *Wyrd* sisters of time, also known as the *Triple Brigittes*, hover in the night sky, holding their fiery arrows as they recite this prayer:

> *"We bring an offering, fine and free*
> *The scent will rise within the Sea*
> *Reach your realms, bless me soon*
> *O Lady of the Darkened Moon"*

While Dawn bravely chooses her time to die and on her own terms, people around the globe suffer another great tragedy on this same historical night. Around 10:50PM, the Lennons' limousine returned to the *Dakota*. John and Yoko got out, passed by an unhinged stalker, and walked towards the archway entrance of the building. Mark Chapman fired five shots from a *.38 Special* revolver, four of which hit Lennon in the back and shoulder, puncturing his left lung and subclavian artery. Lennon was pronounced dead at 11:07PM at *St. Luke's-Roosevelt Hospital Center*, and so marked the end of the Peace Movement.

As Dawn sinks deeper into her watery grave, the news of John Lennon's senseless murder is broadcasted over the radio and television airwaves, thereby causing the rest of the planet to join Cheri in her misery and loss. New Yorkers weren't the only ones who were robbed of a great leader that night, which would be the same date that the beautiful and magical Dawn would be swept away.

The next morning, Cheri awoke to the childish artwork and the devastating note, which explained that Dawn *couldn't handle life anymore* and that *Reuben was waiting for her on the other side*. Cheri had just awoken from a nightmare, where she dreamed that Dawn had died and was walking up the stairway to Heaven, as the Bob Dylan song, *Knocking on Heaven's Door*, played in the background. Panicking and thinking the worst, she ran outside their building and called out Dawn's name, knowing there would be no answer.

A rainbow had come up with the sun, as if serving as a metaphysical bridge between Earth and Heaven. It tormented Cheri to not know what Dawn had done to herself or what had become of her. For all she knew, her precocious kitten had gotten lost on the dark side of the moon and was crying for help. Cheri tells herself that her Cherokee ladylove would be okay, that she was going to a better place, and would soon be floating on the clouds like delicate flower pedals. This was what she told herself, but believing it was an entirely different challenge altogether.

Dawn had been subjected to so much trauma, that it was only inevitable that she would crack. As Cheri wept for her lost lover, sitting on the bed in their small but sensational apartment, she heard a voice that came out of nowhere…a voice that she didn't recognize.

"You were once dead," it told her. "Ephesians 2:1." That was it. That was all the voice had to offer. A voice that she couldn't identify, but evidently felt the urge to reach out to her and console her with an incredibly vague message. Was this supposed to comfort her or terrify her? She'd never know.

A funeral was held for Dawn at the Parisian river where she was last seen, and Cheri was the sole attendant and celebrant. Because her body was never found, Cheri placed a single rock in the vacant coffin as a substitute for Dawn's absent corpse. The secondary function of the rock was intended to *fix the Double*. She believed, as many did, in autoscopy, which was the perception that the *double* (or werewolf) was a spitting image but a separate entity.

Cheri was worried because legend had it that if a werewolf died without curing or ridding itself first, that they would be doomed to endlessly wander between the world of the living and the realm of the dead for as long as their body failed to receive a proper ritual burial. Had Dawn's body been found, Cheri would have smudged it with sage and holy water to bring peace to her soul by casting out and separating the werewolf. Because Dawn had disappeared without a trace, this was not a possible option, and it terrified Cheri to think that it might rob her of her rightful place in eternity.

Was their relationship all for nothing? Had the connection they built gone down the drain? Little did Cheri know that when Dawn died, she found herself outside of her body and in front of a projected beam of bright light. As Dawn began to walk towards the welcoming light, it was suddenly contaminated with a black mist, as if both eternities were vying for her immortal soul.

As Cheri fretted over Dawn's mortality, it subsequently brought to attention her own fate. She knew that being half succubus wasn't going to make good marks with the heavenly Father. She not only feared the prospect of Hell, but it terrified her to envision her afterlife without Dawn. She saw Dawn for the heart she had, not what she had done, and with that in mind, she knew that Heaven wouldn't be Heaven without her. Cheri, at that moment, prayed to God and renounced any lingering connection that she may have had to the dark side, knowingly or unknowingly. As Cheri did this, a hidden force sadistically attacks the repentant Cambion, blinding her like a bat. For too long, she couldn't see what really mattered, and now it looked like she'd never see what was to come.

Cheri sipped on a glass of traditional French wine, which was dry, light, crisp, and had notes of summer berries and grapefruit. She thought back to the days of crying over her mother that she never knew and the slew of foster homes she had become so familiar with. No pyramid scheme could ever fill the holes in her heart, which had been widening and expanding since childhood. Dawn had fulfilled her, and was better than she could have ever asked for, but Dawn had become a blight on her own dismal existence. Dawn's heart was too big for this world, and this world had been no match for her wrath. Cheri continued to drink down the red wine, now gulping it like there was no tomorrow, as if daring the universe to try and intervene.

"What do you got next for me, God?" she asked rhetorically, knowing that whatever it was, it would be bad. "It's alright, Cheri. At least it can't get any worse," she said, talking to herself. "Oh, yes it can…and it will."

DECEMBER 8, 1983
MOOT MOON

It had been three years to the day since Dawn drowned herself in the Seine River. It was a cold and miserable afternoon, so Cheri had chosen to remain indoors. She hadn't dated since Dawn's tragic passing, as she had sworn off love altogether. She just had nothing left to offer, and even if she did, she knew she could never replace Dawn, nor would she want to. She spent most of her days in cataleptic sleep, unaware that Wolf was there snuggling with her. When she wasn't languid or rigid, she spent her time weeping and drinking. She would never get used to being blind, but she did learn to live with it. She worried about Dawn's eternity, wishing that she could be a proxy and intercede for her Indian sweetheart, but considering that Cheri was bred for Hell herself…standing in for Dawn was sadly nothing more than a pipe dream. She ached for her late lover, as her devotion and commitment to Dawn were perennial.

Cheri had the radio on, as she unknowingly laid in bed with Wolf, not able to handle the sounds of silence anymore. Pat Benatar's hit single, *Shadows of the Night*, came on the *FM* station. Halfway through the song, the music turned to white noise. Cheri didn't feel like getting up, but the noise was annoying, so she made herself get out of bed. As she moved to adjust the dial, she heard something that knocked her off her feet and spooked both herself and the wandering spirit of her inherited companion.

"Cheri?" the faded but familiar voice called over the air. "Cheri?"

Wolf's endearing spirit immediately perked his head up and began whimpering, while staring intently at the radio that sat atop of her dresser. Cheri quickly put her ear to the built-in speakers, so as not to miss anything, while tears rushed and streamed down her face.

"Dawn?" Cheri asked, suddenly endowed with hope. "Is that you, baby?"

"I'm sorry," the voice answered back, still and soft.

The voice sounded distant, and was a bit difficult to hear as clearly as she would have liked, but Cheri knew it was her and so did Wolf. Chills ran up Cheri's spine and her skin became overwhelmed with goosebumps. Her body began to shake violently, beyond her control. She waited eagerly to hear Dawn's voice again, but nothing further was coming through the speakers.

"Dawn?!" she shouted in desperation. "Are you there? Dawn?!"

In her manic distress, Cheri picked up the radio and shook it so hard that she lost her balance and fell on the floor again, still holding the radio in her trembling hands.

"I'm sorry," the still voice said again, amidst the white noise. Cheri noticed, at that moment, that the cord had been pulled out of the electrical socket. Her radio had no batteries inside it, so the wall had been its only source of power. Yet, the radio was still on and Dawn was still there.

"Dawn?!" Cheri called out again. "Are you okay? Baby?! I miss you," she said, hysterically sobbing. "I'm here. I love you, Dawn!"

It doesn't even occur to Cheri to tell Dawn what happened to her eyesight, as Dawn's safety is literally all she cares about. Wolf let out a short howl to let Dawn know how sad he was without her. Cheri heard him, which spooked her even more, since she couldn't see him. Wolf had a chance to walk into the beam of light when he died, but he couldn't bear to leave Dawn or Cheri. Now that Dawn had passed away too, he was dying for that bright light to come back for him. There were several minutes of dead air, within the white noise, before the fading voice finally replied.

"I love you both more than you'll ever know," the familiar voice answered, referring to Cheri and Wolf. "I'm sorry. I'm so sorry."

The white noise and the gentle voice both went away as quickly as they came, returning the radio to the station's broadcast, which was now playing the song,

Burnin' For You, by Blue Oyster Cult. Was Dawn in Hell? Was she in limbo? It began to rain outside, not just a drizzle, but a storm. Cheri then felt something on the center of her forehead that was new and different. She reached up with her left hand and discovered that she had miraculously developed a third eye. She turned and discovered yet another wonder, seeing Wolf sitting on her bed.

"I can see you," she told him, as she cried profusely for Dawn. "Wolf…I can see you!" Cheri's vision had suddenly returned, but only in black and white. She had gone from being entirely blind to completely color-blind, but could now see spirits.

Cheri sat on the bed, next to Wolf, feeling him affectionately lick her nose, as she hugged and held his phantom close, while she wept for Dawn. The radio remained unplugged and Cheri would stay broken. She considered committing arson and sticking her head in the fire, to try and see Hell, so she could look for her lost love and make sure she wasn't there. She knew, however, that this wouldn't work and that she was in her own Hell now. Cheri's face began to twitch and convulse, as she blinked hard, ground her teeth, clenched her fists, shifted her jaw, and picked at her face. These ticks were all symptomatic of her becoming a basket case over fretting about her deeply missed and dearly departed lover.

The euphoria of regaining her eyesight was fleeting, as her increasing and growing worry for Dawn immensely overshadowed the relief of having her vision returned. The dead people around her, as well as those in Cheri's own head, became overwhelming, so she bought a *Sony* Walkman from the local record store and used the earphones to drown out the many voices.

Cheri and Wolf revisited Dawn's grave one more time to erect a large cross, which she lifted from *Schoppner's War Cemetery* (where she had to kill the nosy, Bavarian groundskeeper). She referred to the stolen, symbolic artifact as the *Wolf Stone*, in uxorious memory of her departed unhinged lover. Cheri played the Jim Croce song, *I'll Have To Say*, in her head, as she fondly remembered her dear Dawn.

As the years passed, residents, travelers, and passers by, were very suspicious about this stone cross and seldom visited this particular locality for that very reason. Cheri looked up and saw an obscure creature perching on Dawn's idiosyncratic tombstone. She immediately recognized it as, *Horus*, a falcon-headed demon who had the sun and moon as his eyes. She had heard tales about how he piloted a crescent-shaped boat, which he named the *Left Eye of Aluzza*, that apparently took damned souls over a vast sea, into the sun, to burn for all eternity.

"Fuck you!" she threatened the chilling monster of the macabre, while Wolf's ghost snarled and growled at the bird-like reaper. "Neither you or your creepy sister, *Circe*, are going to weave our destiny or spin our fate. Fuck, no!! Be gone, demon! Leave me and my Dawn alone!"

As Cheri left the gravesite for the last time, she listened to her *Ozzy Osbourne* mixtape on her portable player. The song, *Mr. Crowley*, played loudly through her wired earphones. As Cheri walked toward her new *Harley-Davidson* motorcycle, she mutated into a 20-year-old version of herself and then split into two different people. There were suddenly two separate, identical women walking one behind the other. The only noticeable difference was that the new Cheri wasn't wearing a headset, nor had a *Walkman* clipped to her belt. The clone could, however, see, feel, taste, smell, think, and hear everything that Cheri could. They were like psychic twins, except they were made from the same flesh rather than the same womb.

They straddled the motorcycle, with the duplicate sitting behind the original, shoving her hands down the front of Cheri's pants and holding onto her crotch instead of tightly hugging her waist from behind. The customized cassette began playing Ozzy's new song, *Bark at the Moon*. Though Cheri would forever feel alone without her Dawn, she now at least had an outlet where she could pleasure herself and meet her carnal needs. Looking as if they were a full decade younger, the interchangeable duo rides off into the sunset, with the wind in their pink hair and their dreams six feet under.

Dawn was gone, but she would never be forgotten. Cheri might never know the answer to where Dawn ended up, but knew that her 21-year-old Cherokee would always be with her. She just hoped that Dawn was at peace and able to be reconnected with her chosen family. This cold world had taken Dawn from her loving arms, but nobody would ever remove Dawn from her heart. Death could never diminish their love, but only cause it to burn brighter. Dawn had spent her final years a killer, and yet, was a far better person than most. Cheri would never get over her loss, but the fact that she had known Dawn at all made her a winner...and a lucky one at that. None of us ever truly die, and Dawn was certainly no exception.

AUGUST 30, 1968

Linda was speaking on the pulpit, passionately preaching against the evils of censorship at a political rally in Columbia, MD. They were about 30 miles from home, at the *Merriweather Post Pavilion*, where *The Doors* were scheduled to play later that evening. This controversial protest was sponsored by *Playboy* Magazine, who were physically represented to support Linda's appreciated contribution. The song, *Hungry*, by Paul Revere & The Raiders, had kicked off the unorthodox sermon.

"Men like Hugh Hefner and Bob Guccione are pioneers, not perverts!" she yelled out at the crowd below her, who cheered and applauded her liberal stance. "What has repression ever done for this country? Nothing but death and destruction! When are we ever going to learn from our own history?!"

Reverend Moon was far away, leading a missions trip in Haiti, trying his best to convert those who embrace Voodoo and Santeria. Dawn's nose was red from using *Kleenex* to tend to her 9-year-old sniffles. Her father was often absent from her life, but somehow the sting of goodbye never got any easier to bear. Even though he always gave her an inappropriate hug before he left, she still trusted that he loved her while he took every opportunity to feel her up and grab her butt. She was a perceptive little girl in some ways, while naïve and gullible in others.

Though she was with her mother that day, you'd never know it. Linda was an absentee parent too, in her own right. Beck Runnel was there, as usual, to keep Dawn company and serve as her diligent guardian. Nobody else could see him, but that didn't stop her from knowing he was real. He appeared to be in his thirties. His face was faintly pale, with a bluish tint. He had wavy, blue hair that ended just past his shoulders and eyes like the ocean. He was a tall, mysterious man draped in a trench coat and top hat. She felt protected by him, which kept her from panicking in her isolation. She knew Linda ignored her, but she had to believe that she was wanted in spite of the neglect and disinterest. Dawn had been left to entertain herself, among the crowd of enthusiasts and activists that had gathered for this public spectacle.

"Fuck," she said quietly to herself, noticing that her frosty treat had gotten on her favorite shirt.

Dawn had been enjoying a waffle cone, containing a double-scoop of her two favorite flavors of *Breyers* ice cream: *Black Cherry* and *Black Raspberry*.

"Now, Dawn," Beck said, as he knelt down to meet her at her level, "is that any way for your Daddy's little Analodi to talk?"

"I guess not," the distraught Dawn said softly, as she slowly shook her head and looked down at the sticky mess on her blouse. "I ruined it," she said, beginning to cry over the spilt ice cream.

"Hey, hey, it's okay," Beck insisted, attempting to console her before she had made an emotional scene. "Dawn, it's okay. You're in good hands," he told her, while he pressed his hands against her undeveloped chest.

Dawn felt wetness produce from his palms. The water was cool and pure, as if coming from a brook in Heaven. The water was also controlled, as it only soaked the part of her shirt that needed attention. When Beck removed his hands, the ice cream stain was gone, like it had never been there.

"1 Corinthians 13:13 says, *the greatest of these is love*," Beck told her. "In this verse, God is telling us that love is a gift that he blesses us with indiscriminately and abundantly. Yet, love...true and unconditional...often only comes to those who only love themselves." he tells her, as if reading her very soul without knowing the first thing about her. "Either that, or God gets off on allowing the tenderhearted to experience love for a brief moment, just before snatching it away or revealing it to be a lie."

"Jeremiah 17:9 tells us that the heart is deceitful and who can know it, but it's the other way around," Dawn educated him, refusing to let Beck kick her while she was down. "It's the heartless who are deceitful, while the rest of us know our hearts very well."

Beck, who was actually a nefarious phantom that manifested from a cloud of darkness, began to sidle in a strange sideways motion. Once he saw that Dawn wasn't afraid of him and no longer afraid to be left alone, he turned and walked away until his body became a puff of black smoke.

"Pornography isn't exploitation of women, but rather celebration of women! Showing our bodies isn't degrading, but liberating!" Linda shouted in front of her microphone, setting a great example for her young and impressionable daughter.

Linda had forgotten that Dawn had even tagged along, showing full devotion to reaching total strangers and little to no concern for Dawn. She liked their daughter, but she didn't want to be tied down with responsibility. She had her own life to live, and though she cared for Dawn, having a child was often a burden and felt like baggage. Mingan would disappear for an undetermined length of time, using the ministry as his excuse. Linda was there more than he was, though her mind and so-called heart were often somewhere else. Both claimed to adore their daughter and regularly made promises they had no plans on keeping. Dawn wanted to feel like her parents wanted to be around her, but the older she got, the more she accepted that this wish would never be granted. Dawn had come to know the vices and indulgences of her parents, especially behind closed doors and thin walls. She knew, deep at her core, that she was more of an obligation than anything else. In spite all this, Dawn still loved her parents, so she played along, consistently saying and doing what they wanted.

Beck saw that she had finished devouring her waffle cone, and that her head was clearly somewhere else. Though he had vanished, he hadn't disappeared. He spoke to her once again.

"Hang in there, Dawn. I'm sure your mother will come and play with you soon," he told her, knowing that Linda had no desire to do so.

Dawn concurs with a silent nodding of her head, as Beck notices a single tear drop down her little cheek. He also sees that she has dried ice cream all over her face. Beck holds out his hands and once again magically makes a pond of water in his open palms. She no longer sees him, but she sees his hands, which are now made of black smoke. While he holds his hands together side by side, Dawn puts her face in them and washes the ice cream off.

The hours got closer to showtime and Linda finally took a break from preaching to the masses. She made a call to one of the elders of their church, instructing him to come and pick up Dawn. Since Linda was there speaking with *Playboy* Magazine, the grateful Pavilion allowed her to use their private phone that was on the premises. Before long, Bob and Teila Sewell, a married couple from the church, arrived to take Dawn off of Linda's hands. They had brought her backpack, which contained her favorite stuffed wolf and the Margaret Wise Brown book, *Goodnight Moon.* These people had access to Dawn's personals because this wasn't nearly the first time that Linda had dumped her off on the reliable congregants.

"Goodbye, honey," Linda said, leaning over and kissing her daughter on the forehead, while holding the sides of her face in her cold and clammy hands. "I'll see you soon, baby. Mommy promises."

Dawn had learned many times that her mother's promises were as empty as they come, but she didn't want to upset or let her mother down. After a moment or two of awkward silence, Dawn met her mother's gaze and reciprocated her fake smile. It was obvious to everyone in the picture that Dawn was pretty low on her mother's priority scale, but the church was there to serve the Moons unconditionally and without question. Besides, Linda had bought her that frozen snack earlier, which kind of made up for abandoning her for yet another selfish escapade. This was what Dawn told herself, anyhow. Whether she actually believed it was another story altogether.

"Okay, Mommy," Dawn responded, numb to the guaranteed expectation of being regularly disappointed by her parents.

Dawn waved goodbye to her mother, as Linda made her classic escape. Linda was overly anxious to get ready for her big night, and now there was nobody in her way to cramp her style.

Linda made haste, getting overdressed for her overdue moment with her magic man. She was soon decorated in a neon orange, gingham crop top that had elastic hitting just under her breasts. This was accompanied by a low-cut, cotton mini skirt that had swirl patterns of baby blue and hot pink. She had added bounce and flair to her long locks, using a curling iron. Her *Max Factor* lipstick was a frosted pink and her heels were turquoise and white. Her *Mary Quant* eye shadow was a lime green, which accentuated her false eyelashes. She had silver skulls for stud-earrings. She completed the look with a black chain belt that hung low on one of her hips, teal go-go boots, and a white leather jacket that draped around her shoulders. She had smothered on the green apple perfume, like she had caked on her overdone cosmetics. One would have thought that she was preparing to meet royalty, the way she looked. Yet, she was determined to hookup with a rock star, not a prince.

It's now moments away from the big event and she found herself standing at the life-changing venue, where she had spent all day. She takes a deep breath and nervously picks at the skirt of her dress. She slowly exhales as she works her way around to find her seat, just barely having time to get situated. She wanted to stay at this outdoor arena forever, sure of herself and confident that things would go her way. She didn't have an after-party laminate around her neck, but she had a body for sin that she knew would win her backstage access.

"Hey, baby. Why don't you bring your happenin' ass this way? We got a seat for ya, right here!" she heard one of the male patrons call out, showing her less shame than she was planning on showing Jim.

The man hitting on her was far from her type and anything but charming, but she was happy to rock his world if he could help her out in return.

"Can you get me to meet Jim?" she flirted, just in case. "I'll suck your tiny cock for the inimitable privilege."

"Well, you're a sweet-talker, aint ya?" he said back sarcastically, while his friends laughed at his expense. "Your father must be proud."

"Yeah, that's what I thought," she said back, refusing to let her rude admirer spoil her special night. This was her chance to stray from the monotonous routine of her daily life. She was enthralled and captivated, and nobody was going to water-down her unrestrained enthusiasm.

It was finally 8:30 and some band that nobody cared about, called *The Earth Opera*, performs as the opening act. Linda squirms in her seat, fighting not to cream her underpants, as it hits her that she is at the *Waiting for*

The Sun tour. This show wasn't sold-out, but there was no shortage of attendance, despite the fact that it was a late addition and not advertised. This was the first of four shows that they were scheduled to play within the next three days. The place was covered in video cameras to tape live footage for the documentary, *Feast of Friends*, which ended up being unusable and shelved. The audience roared and applauded as the opening act took a bow, not because they were good, but because they were leaving. Linda got goosebumps and chewed her nails, while band equipment was switched out and amplifiers were plugged in.

The Doors were a bit late coming on stage, but this delay was sort of expected. Jim was notorious for making the masses wait around on him, while he indulges in his pre-show boffs with groupies. Linda begins to drum her fingers against her quivering knees, anxious and impatient for the show to begin, as her whiskey sits under her seat. She couldn't help but breathe in the suffocating aroma of sex, as most of the women stripped and masturbated right where they were. The anticipation of seeing Jim overcame them, and his procrastination only made them more hot and bothered between their legs. Linda was neither pleased or impressed with Jim's behavior, but it didn't make her desire him any less.

"Is everybody in? Is everybody in? The ceremony is about to begin," Morrison's mindless voice announces, from what appears to be out of nowhere. "The show will begin in 5 minutes. All those unseated will await the next show. The program for this evening is not new, you've seen this entertainment through and through. You've seen your birth, your life, and death, you might recall all of the rest. Did you have a good world when you died, enough to base a movie on?" Jim's voice vibrated through the outdoor auditorium, which was vast and silent.

The lights dim and the audience cheers, standing to greet their stoned shaman. Jim finally arrives, stumbling awkwardly onto the stage. He is introduced as, *Dionysus*, and asks that he be addressed as such. His paying worshippers don't mind his drugged stupor, as they are seeing psychedelic imagery themselves. The whole place was tripping on acid and other narcotics. The cluster of security was too sauced to notice or care.

It didn't matter to Linda that Jim was a staggering and obnoxious drunkard. Her eyes swelled up with tears as she imagined him taking her to *Love Street* and having his way with her. She believed she just needed a minute alone with him to monopolize and fulfill his craving. Linda was just a drop in the bucket when it came to those who had an obsessive crush on Morrison, yet she knew she'd have a chance if she could only catch his eye. She was just as foxy as any groupie he'd serviced before, and her willingness would make her irresistible.

Jim opened the set list with, *Back Door Man*. Linda had been dying to see *The Doors* play live, ever since she could remember. She sings along, at the top of her lungs, losing herself in the lyrics. Linda loved this song in particular, as it was about the anal sex she had grown to love. She had brought *Jack Daniels* with her, hoping to share it with Jim. There was still plenty left, but she drank enough to feel the blunt repercussions. She longed for him to whisk her away on a moonlight drive, where they'd spend the rest of their lives in passion. As he sang his poetic lyrics and tried to maintain his balance, all the chicks in the audience lost their inhibitions and threw their bras and panties on stage, climbing over each other to try and get him to look their direction. This chaos blocked Linda from seeing Jim, so she tried to break through the stockade of sluts, only to feel a sharp blow to the back of the head and watch her vision go dark. Linda had fallen into the dogpile of insane superfans, being trampled on and kicked, as she lay there limp and motionless on the ground.

The *Doors* had gotten halfway through their set. Jim began singing, *The Crystal Ship*, which he started in the wrong key. He suddenly felt ill, with a deep sickness that he couldn't quite put his finger on. His three friends assumed it was due to his habitual binge drinking, but it was something else this time. Ray quickly grabbed the trash can and slid it over to Jim, who puked a few times, ridding his system of most of the booze. He then shakily stood back up and edged toward the rim of the stage, sensing that something was wrong. The mood suddenly changed, as the audience shifted from cheering Jim on to screaming in horror. Jim yelled at the crowd, demanding that they show him what had happened. They obediently complied and as they scattered, Jim saw her lying still and sullied on the floor. The dots slowly began to connect in his state of haze, while he exploded with emotion. Linda had been the victim of a human stampede. She was bloodied and battered from being stomped and treaded on by all the heels of Jim's unruly demographic.

The show was cut short and never finished. Jim wanted to escort the girl to the hospital himself, but was robbed of this honor. Ray, John, and Robbie did their best to move their singer through the walls of anarchy, so they could promptly chase the ambulance. On the ride there, the band felt devastated at the idea of one of their concerts ending in a fatality, which was unacceptable.

"Linda?! Linda?! Where the fuck is Linda Moon?!" Jim inquired with genuine concern, demanding to be told, as he clumsily made his way through the hospital.

Morrison finally found Linda's room and gently swung the door open, only to catch more than one doctor sexually assaulting his injured fan. Her clothes had been pulled up or torn, leaving her exposed. Not willing to believe what he was seeing, Jim took a step back and reevaluated the situation. They were taking turns violating and defiling her, using this opportunity to their advantage while she was still completely out of it. Jim was startled and spooked by this, but was not about to stand by and let it happen.

"Easy, man. If you want some that bad, just get in line," one of the three MD's said, noticing Jim standing there and looking like he was into it. The doctor reveled in watching his dirty colleague enjoy the sedated patient. "She's a choice little mink, ain't she?" he asked, while massaging the bulge in his pants.

This offensive assumption only further enraged Jim. He could see them for what they were, which was the stuff nightmares are made from. Their teeth were like carpentry nails, their eyes were solid black, and their skin looked like it was inside out. The doctor moaned as he relentlessly continued to plow into her, not being the slightest disturbed or dissuaded by Jim's presence. These wicked sounds became grunts and gasps, as the trusted professional nears the edge of climaxing, drilling into her from behind.

"Proverbs 6:16-19 tells us that the Lord detests a haughty person who lies, kills, devises wicked schemes, and takes pleasure from harming others! You cocksuckers are all zombies!" the lizard king screamed at the baleful professionals.

Jim closes the door behind him, as he feels a switch turn on inside him. He landed blow after blow, yelling incoherently at the three doctors as he pounded their flesh. Jim took a break, only to pull her dress down and close her legs. There were Native American spirits there who tried to help him, but he angrily swatted them away. The tribal ghosts knew Jim well enough to not argue, so they wisely gave him the space he needed. Jim resumed mercilessly beating the spoiled predators, until Ray rushed in and pulled the rock idol off before homicide could be added to his list of accomplishments. Jim slumped over to Linda, smoothed her hair down, and cried like a baby. Ray crouched down and checked for a pulse, making sure that the three doctors were still breathing.

Jim waited for the three physicians to be taken away by the police, and made sure that they were replaced with upstanding ones. They examined and treated Linda, while Ray waited for Jim outside the room. After another couple of hours, the drugs began to wear off and Linda started to come out of her bad trip. She slowly noticed that she was in the *ER* and was shocked to see that her hero was kneeling at her bedside.

"Jim? Jim Morrison?" she asked, delightfully amazed by his welcomed company. "Jim?" she asked again, not fully willing to believe her own eyes.

Once she gathered herself enough to accept that she was in his presence, she asked Jim what had happened, only he didn't have the heart to tell her. Without speaking a word, Jim stood up and kissed her on the forehead. She gently laid her hand on his arm, as she happily breathed in his overwhelming aroma of whiskey and body odor.

"You're not leaving, are you? Please, Jim, can't you stay with me?" she begged, still having no clue that she had been gang raped.

"Linda," Jim said, "my symmetrical angel. I'll always be with you."

"I'm scared, Jim. I'm scared to go back out there. I hate this country. People are evil."

"I know about heartache and the loss of God. Sometimes, we must wear terrifying and monstrous masks in order to inscribe ourselves on the hearts of humanity. You're a groovy chick, Linda. If the stars were aligned in our favor, I could see myself being stuck on you. I really could."

"Please," she begged again, "don't leave me. I just found you. I finally found you."

"This life is just a dream, Linda. It's just a dream."

Linda reluctantly let go of his arm and as she did, Jim vanished into thin air, while a small lizard magically appeared on the back of her hand. The three doctors never went to jail or lost their careers.

The *Doors* didn't want this story leaking out to the press, so they paid off the media to pretend that it never happened. Instead, legend has it that the concert played through 'til the End, literally. Allegedly, when they came back for the encore, Jim asked the audience which song they'd rather hear for the finale, *The Unknown*

Soldier or *The End*. The crowd roared louder for the latter, hoping that it would keep Morrison on stage longer. Jim grabbed the microphone and shrieked, as only Morrison could.

"Turn off the fucking lights!" he shouted in an authoritative and dominant tone, as the entire pavilion was plunged into darkness. That's how they say that night happened, but those who were actually there know otherwise.

Meanwhile, Dawn is waiting for her mother to come pick her up from the babysitter's. Like usual, Dawn was plopped down in front of the television, completely ignored and neglected. The *News* is on, talking about a vampire cult that is facing life sentences. Among the convicted is a 32-year-old man named, Reuben Ian Peterson. The cult followed expert-brainwasher, Rodrick Stovall, who was 50-years-old but believed himself to be a 500-year-old vampire named, *Oberath*. This cult was solely responsible for one of the most blood-curdling, home invasion murders in history.

The victims were Bradley and Gale Charm. Their daughter, Charity, was a long-time friend of Stovall's who had recently ran away from home. She had described her home life as 'a living hell,' which Stovall decided to take it upon himself to fix. Stovall and fellow clan member, Carlton Rogers, entered the Floridian, suburban home through their unlocked garage. Charity waited outside the house, while Reuben waited in the getaway car. Once inside, Carlton wrangled up and restrained the unsuspecting spouses. Rod then beat both Bradley and Gale to death with a crowbar, and then feasted on the married couple's blood. Rod even made some sandwiches with the bread and eggs he found in their kitchen, using the couple's blood as a condiment.

After the deed was done, Stovall, along with Rogers, Peterson, and Charity, fled to the swamps of Louisiana, to evade and escape the police. Luckily, the authorities had been tipped off by Charity's psychic Aunt, who could see the clan's location. They were arrested in Baton Rouge, not long after arriving there. All four members were extradited to Florida, to collectively and separately stand trial for their parts in the brutal murders. Stovall immediately plead guilty to the murder of Gale and Bradley. The remaining members were also found accountable and sentenced. For a time, Rod Stovall was the youngest American prisoner ever on death row. His sentence was commuted to 2,000 years, with the possibility of parole in 20. Rogers also received a life sentence for his essential role in the murders. Peterson was granted a suspended sentence for his incriminating testimony. Charity received 10.5 years and hung herself in prison.

"I understood myself only after destroying myself."

- Sade Andria Zabala

"Sex is like an atom bomb. A potent weapon which fascinates and frightens. We're afraid to let it loose, yet we all have our finger on the button."

- Zeena Schreck

ABOUT THE AUTHOR

Nicholas Knight is the doting father to two beautiful daughters, Rose and Harley. He lost Rose to a devastating miscarriage and then lost Harley to (her mother's) spite and selfishness. Sadly, neither of the two mothers turned out to reciprocate his affection or devotion. To his delight, he was able to reconcile with Rose's mother, 25 years later, who ended up being as sweet as he remembered (even though she didn't want him). In the end, he would only ever be loved back by one very special woman, whom he would lose tragically to his own foolishness and her heart-wrenching suicide. Nicholas is twice divorced to two monumental and malignant mistakes, neither of whom are the mothers of his daughters or the heavenly love of his life.

Taking his painful history into consideration, nobody would have ever expected or anticipated Nicholas to write such endearing stories about a charming heroine. Yet, by some miracle, he was able to create, *Dawn*, who has very much become his third daughter. Nicholas has a big heart, though it has been relentlessly and repeatedly shattered, and this heart of gold shows in his extraordinary writing. This erotic-werewolf trilogy is a brilliant work of fiction, but those few who intimately know Nicholas, know that there is a lot of hidden reality in this legend of fantasy.

Nicholas resides in the secluded Blue Ridge Mountains of Virginia, with his best friend, Tiger, and the lovely spirit of his forever soulmate, the enchanting and unforgettable, Erica. Determined to make something of himself and to make his kids proud, he chases his pipe dream of becoming a successful author and actor. He pursues these unattainable passions, notwithstanding the overabundance of monsters who would kill to see him fail and fade away (much like his final and lethal ex-wife, Heather, who proved to be a sinister and sadistic ruse). As this cruel world continues to do everything in its power to see Nicholas defeated and forsaken, he carries on through the endless storms, praying that the day will finally come where God will allow him to have his due.

He has tried several times, over the years, to break into the ministry, but the Christian church always found it more entertaining to condemn, censure, and crucify him. Nicholas is a very spiritual person, and has a real heart for children, animals, and the homeless. One would think that the Christian community would have honored and rewarded such a benevolent heart, but sadly, the Christian church is not Christian (as he has learned time and time again).

Thank you for supporting this sentimental saga, and for reading Dawn's sensual and sensational series. Hopefully, you have been deeply touched by Dawn's exciting and exceptional testimony, as we have. Never forget what (or who) really matters, and never let them go. Don't let this brutally cold world demolish and destroy you, and always remember that the only thing worth living for…and dying for…is love. Peace be with you all. Be different. Be kind.

You can contact Nicholas at:

harleysdaddy06@gmail.com

His acting CV/resume can be viewed at:

www.imdb.me/nicholasknight

The *Amazon* links to his books can be found here:

www.facebook.com/nightshadenovels

He also has a *YouTube* Channel:

www.youtube.com/user/twilighthaven13

WOLF PRESERVES & RESCUES:

Wolves, like most of God's majestic creatures, are (and have long been) in real danger of extinction, courtesy of the overabundance of bloodthirsty hunters, poachers, fighters, and otherwise ammosexuals. There are a few sanctuaries within this violent country, who actually have the decency to care about these innocent and defenseless souls.

- Seacrest Wolf Preserve; 3449 Bonnett Pond Rd, Chipley, FL 32428-3828; 850-773-2897 www.seacrestwolfpreserve.org

- Howling Woods Farm; 1371 W Veterans Hwy, Jackson, NJ 08527; 609-901-1387 luv2howl@optonline.net.

If you want to visit a sanctuary that is a bit more guarded, where you would look but not touch the wolves, see the two listed below. This way is more impersonal, since you'd be seeing the wolves through a wire fence, but I hear good things about these rescues nonetheless:

- Wolf Sanctuary of PA; 465 Speedwell Forge Rd, Lititz, PA 17543; 717-626-4617 https://wolfsanctuarypa.org

- Lakota Wolf Preserve; 89 Mount Pleasant Road, Columbia, NJ 07832; 908-496-9244 www.lakotawolf.com

Also by Nicholas Knight:

NICHOLAS
KNIGHT

E DEPARTMENT

Detective Bureau

on Measurements

Head Length,	L. Foot,
Head Width,	Mid. F.
Len	Lit. F.
	Fore A.

THE
NIGHTSHADE SERIES
DAWN'S TALE

Also by Nicholas Knight: